BELOW
LUCK
LEVEL

Barbara Erasmus

CATALYST PRESS
EL PASO, TEXAS, USA

For further information, write info@catalystpress.org

In North America, this book is distributed by
Consortium Book Sales & Distribution, a division of Ingram.
Phone: 612/746-2600
cbsdinfo@ingramcontent.com
www.cbsd.com

In South Africa, Namibia, and Botswana,
this book is distributed by Protea Distribution.
For information, email orders@proteadistribution.co.za.

FIRST EDITION
10 9 8 7 6 5 4 3 2 1

ISBN 978-1960803030

Library of Congress Control Number: 2024936395

...she lives

Below luck level, never imagining some lottery

Will change her load of pottery to wings.

— KAY RYAN —

BELOW LUCK LEVEL

Barbara Erasmus

She was dead when I woke up beside her the next morning.

I wasn't immediately certain she was dead. I'd never seen a dead person before. She looked just like herself. As if she were sleeping. Her eyes were shut, the white sheet still folded neatly under her chin, exactly as she'd been when I switched off the bedside light the night before, praying I'd somehow fall asleep myself. But I registered a stillness in the room.

"Mom?" I asked tentatively. "Mom, are you awake?"

She was dead, so she said nothing.

"Mom?" Dread snaked through my veins like icy water. My fingers reached out and touched her face, almost of their own volition. They recoiled defensively, like a curling centipede. Was it her coldness? Or the lack of movement?

"Mom!" I pulled back the sheet and shook her. "Mom!

Are you all right?" Recoiled again – at the stiffness this time? I shook her once again before I knew the truth. My shaking fingers snatched up my cell phone from the bedside table. I punched in D. Dial D for Dave. Double D for Dr. Dave.

He answered almost immediately. Perhaps you're programmed to do that if you know you're the doctor on call. Even if it's not yet morning. I started crying when I heard his voice. I wanted to speak, but my words were drowning. I couldn't haul them to the surface.

"Hello?" he said again. "Who is this?"

"She's dead," I said at last. "I think she's dead."

"Who is this?" he repeated. I could hear the urgency in his voice, the note of concern that was his trademark. He was intrinsically compassionate. I found the words to tell him who I was. Who she was.

"It's Hannah," I said. "My mother's not moving. She's so cold. I think she may be dead."

"Hannah," he said at once. "I'm coming, Hannah. I'm on my way."

"But what must I do?" I asked despairingly. "What must I do until you get here?"

"Stay with her, Hannah," he said gently. "Just sit beside her. I'll be with you soon. Just sit beside her until I come."

I couldn't put the phone down when he rang off. I clutched it like a lifebelt, but the silence persuaded me that it was pointless. I replaced the handset carefully on the bedside table, as if it were made of fragile porcelain. I didn't want to break my link to Dave because he was the doctor. He would intervene. He would know how to replay the hours between then and now.

I sat down beside her. I don't know how much time passed. It seemed interminable. I tried to stroke her hair, but I flinched at the coldness of her face. I thought I should run a bath. To warm her. Or make some tea. I thought I should perhaps make a cup of tea, to pass the time until the doorbell rang. But I couldn't get up to switch the kettle on while she lay there. I couldn't leave her all alone.

I looked at her quiet face against the white pillow. A sliver of early morning sun sidled in and settled across her features. It made her look faded. As if she were wearing a worn-out version of my mother's face. I wanted to shut out the sunlight, but I was rooted to the bed. I couldn't get up to close the gap in the curtains.

It seemed a long time before the doorbell rang.

➤

ONE

I stole the last copy of *Books & Leisure* because it had a review of my mother's contribution to struggle literature, and I knew she'd want it for her scrapbook. I scrabbled around in my purse for fifty rand, but I didn't have enough. I'd squandered my remaining cash on carrot cake and a cappuccino, which I'd wolfed down with my usual gusto in the café above the bookstore.

I really wanted the magazine, so I took it. Shoplifting becomes habitual if you get away with it for as long as I have. I hadn't stolen anything for years but the slide-it-into-the-rucksack routine was part of my psyche by then. The sleight of hand required was second nature. Bookshops are easy targets for us experienced kleptomaniacs. They're not geared up for smash-and grab-clientele. Their customers are like my mother: they drop in to browse through the books in a civilized manner. It feels almost unethical to steal in those circumstances, but I suppose they must budget for the occasional aberration like me.

When I got home, I cut out the review to paste it on a new page in her scrapbook. I'd officially taken charge of her scrapbook since my return from London. She seemed too disorganised to do it herself. I skimmed through the review before I stuck it on the page. It was too literary for me to read in detail – something about her skill with characterization, her ability to capture both the angst and promise of the years before we turned into a democracy. It was a double-page feature with cover photos of all five of her novels and the standard portrait which all the reviewers seem to use. Her hair looked a bit wild but elegance had never been her style. I was proud of her.

I noticed a single column about an American poet on the back of the book review before I applied the glue. Kay Ryan. I'd never heard of her, but she'd apparently won some accolade. I glanced at the extract they quoted. It was quite short, but random lines lodge in my mind like barnacles.

...She lives
Below luck-level, never imagining some lottery
Will change her load of pottery to wings

The words struck a chord. I dipped below luck level all the time. I always joined the slowest queue at Pick n Pay. My list of men who'd failed to develop into long-term relationships grew longer every year. I was deep below luck level on the day I stole the magazine. I'd had a string of elated emails from my best friends, crammed with spicy updates about their long-term relationships.

Julia, Mary and I had been inseparable since school-days. Over the years, we'd hunted as a pack, buoyed by the conviction that that there was a knight in shining armor waiting in the wings for each of us. We knew it was just a matter of time before we tracked him down. The fun of the chase diminished when my UK visa expired before theirs did. I had to break ranks and leave them behind in London. They hunted on without me and sure enough their knights in shining armor emerged from the traffic. Julia was engaged to hers. Mary's must have shed his armor at some stage, because she'd just discovered the alarming news that she was pregnant. I'd done some hunting on my own in Cape Town and latched onto Daniel, but I saw him as a stop-gap – he was more like a third best friend than a knight in shining armor.

>

Julia wanted to get married in her family mansion in Oranjezicht so her parents flew her home for the occasion. Mary and I were both bridesmaids. She was so newly pregnant that there was no problem with flying back from London. It felt like old times as the wedding plans came together.

I must have drunk at least a vat of wine at the hen party, which perhaps explains why I felt so deep below luck level when I surfaced beside Daniel the next morning.

I hunched sullenly under the sheets. I didn't even say goodbye when he went off to work. I couldn't confess to anyone how despairing I felt at the prospect of Julia's wedding. I was twenty-nine years old. I already had three bridesmaid's dresses – which I refused to wear again – and now I had to organize a bloody baby shower for Mary. It was too much to handle.

Not that I wanted a baby. Or even a bridegroom, for that matter. But I was starting to think that there was zero prospect of either. And that didn't suit me very well. One likes to be single and childless by choice.

I get dreadful headaches in direct proportion to my intake of red wine. I felt suicidal when I opened my bathroom cabinet and found that my packet of Syndol was empty. I forced myself into my jeans and drove the short distance to the chemist. As soon as the assistant gave it to me, I ripped open the replacement packet and wolfed the pills down like an addict. I had to ask her to bring me a glass of water. I can't swallow Syndol without water. They're big and yellow and bitter, but I was desperate to relieve my headache and now the pills were stuck in my throat.

A cellphone began to ring annoyingly in the handbag of the woman standing next to me. A well-groomed woman. She looked rich. Jewish. She made me aware of how scruffy I was in my none-too-spotless jeans and shapeless T-shirt. Answer the bloody phone, I thought sourly to myself as the Syndol stuck in my throat. I was afraid I was going to throw up on the counter. The woman found her phone and began to talk extremely loud. I hate people who talk on their cell phones out in public. I wished I had a revolver in my handbag. It's so easy to annoy me on a below-luck-level day.

"Oh, it went really well!" she gushed. "It was the most wonderful wedding! The Vineyard is a fantastic venue, and she looked too beautiful! They both did! What a couple! And Isaac's little girls were too enchanting! They danced as much as the rest of us!"

She went on to say that the lucky couple had flown off to some private game reserve for their honeymoon. It really pissed me off. I'm sick of lucky couples. Her family had more than its share of luck, I thought resentfully as I watched the teller process her Lotto ticket. It triggered a memory of the magazine I'd stolen a month before. Kay Ryan's poem mentions a lottery which prompted me to fill in a Lotto ticket of my own while I drank the water.

Swapping the tickets once they'd been printed was a completely random decision.

The over-lucky lady put hers down on the counter with her other purchases when she reached to get out her purse. She was still talking on her cell so she wasn't paying full attention. My own ticket was lying next to hers on top of the open box of Syndol. I didn't know yet that I'd decided to swap them. My hand reached out, purely of its own volition, in a replay of my first successful heist all those years ago. My hand had learned new cunning by this time. I didn't leave it to chance that she would continue to look away. I created a diversion.

My eyes were as shifty as ever. There was a substantial pile of energy bars, arranged artistically beside the till. I knocked them all over the counter and made a last-minute decision to send my glass of water flying too. Chaos on the counter. Mission accomplished.

"Ooh, I'm so sorry!" I gushed insincerely as I mopped up the water and bundled the energy bars into a pile, along with the lucky lady's tissues and my Syndol. And the Lotto tickets. She was still talking on her cell. She made no effort to help, so it served her right. I switched the Lotto tickets with my usual deftness. Tricky Fingers Hannah. I could probably get a job in a circus.

"Mustn't get these wet!" I cried thrusting my ticket into her hand. She didn't even look at the numbers. She was fussing around because some water had spilled on her skirt. People hate to get wet. The glass of water was a winner.

"Don't worry, dear!" said the chemist. My heart was pounding as I picked up my Syndol and left the shop. I thought of gobbling down the entire packet when I got to the carpark. I was all in a tizz. I half expected the over-lucky lady to materialize at my window and demand her ticket back. I'd done it all on impulse, and I was already feeling guilty. Maybe I should track her down and warn her that her luck had changed? Maybe I should go back to the chemist?

But maybe I should just go home. I told my heart to stop beating. The chances of her winning the Lotto were about as high as me attending a batchelorette party of my own. Nothing would come of it. I switched on the engine and drove home.

But I didn't throw the ticket away.

➤

I never watch the Lotto draw. I usually forget to buy a ticket and when I do, I store it in such a safe place that I can never find it again. But this was different. Later that day, I looked up the number for the national office to ask if there was a live broadcast.

The receptionist sounded very patronizing when she heard my query – as if it was a question everyone should be able to answer. She seemed to take it for granted that the entire nation would be glued to e.tv on Wednesday and Saturday evenings at nine-thirty. I was tempted to point out that the entire nation doesn't yet have electricity.

But I said nothing. I didn't want to draw attention to myself. What if she remembered the call?

I was being ridiculous. Sherlock Holmes himself could never track me down. Daniel was the one I should have been worried about.

"Why on earth are you interested in the Lotto broadcast?" he asked me when I put the phone down. I hadn't heard him come home.

"I need to watch this particular draw," I admitted.

"Why?" he asked disbelievingly." Do you think you might win? Have you had some sort of vision?"

"Well, I might win. Anyone could win," I pointed out.

"But no one ever does," he said. "What's so special about this draw? Why do you even have a ticket?

"I stole it," I said brashly. "I never win anything. I thought my luck might change if I stole someone else's."

"You stole the ticket?" he asked incredulously. "How could you steal a ticket? Who did you steal it from?"

He didn't know I was a well-established felon. No-one mentions theft in a job application. Now that I was an adult, I paid for what I wanted – unless I happened to be low on petty cash.

But I'd developed another reckless habit. I always told Daniel everything, so I told him about Kay Ryan's poem. About feeling below luck level. About being the only one not getting married. About being the only one not having a baby.

This wasn't my wisest decision. Daniel was furious.

"So you're saying that being with me makes you feel less lucky than Jules and Mary? Being with me makes you feel so unlucky that you deserve to win the Lotto as compensation?"

"No!" I protested, waving my hands ineffectually in the air. "I love being with you! But they're getting married. Or having babies. It feels as if they're leaving me behind."

I knew the conversation was going nowhere. Daniel was very keen on marriage. He was eager to sire an entire herd of babies. He couldn't understand why I refused to consider either option. I didn't really understand it myself. Neither did my mother who was never reticent about giving her opinion.

She was even angrier than Daniel when she heard about the stolen ticket. Even she knew nothing about my thieving past. God knows why I mentioned the Lotto ticket when she dropped in the next morning. Maybe I saw it more as a swap than a fully fledged theft.

"You are tempting the gods!" she warned me. "There are Greek myths written about people like you who play with fire and end up roaming around in hell forever!"

"All right! All right! I'll throw the blood thing away!" I yelled, flinging the ticket theatrically into the dustbin. I put the kettle on to make some tea in a martyred manner. We were all silent as we watched the kettle boil.

"Maybe we should check out the draw on Wednesday," my mom suggested cautiously.

"Just as a matter of interest..." added Daniel.

I felt a surge of relief. I emptied the dustbin on the kitchen floor and dug feverishly through the potato peels and tea bags. The ticket was damp and unsavoury when I pounced upon it, but it wasn't irrevocable. I read out the numbers.

"Twelve. Nineteen. Thirty. Thirty-one. Forty-six. Forty-eight."

My mother returned to Daniel's house for the draw. The three of us lined up on the sofa half an hour early. The chances of winning might have been miniscule, but miniscule is not a synonym for zero.

➤

I remember the hoopla when Mbeki launched the first national lottery in South Africa at the start of the new millennium. It was against the religion of the old regime, as far as I remember. Like drinking on Sundays or having sex with colored strangers.

I'd fiddled around on Google that afternoon, just to

pass the time. I'd researched the possibilities of winning. There are multiple statistics that show that it's virtually impossible to win the lottery, even if you buy a ticket with religious fervour every week. There are no magic formulae. No brilliant professors have come up with a foolproof plan. You need six winning numbers from a field of forty-nine. The odds are one in fourteen million. Multiple tickets don't seem to be a solution. Even if you spend over twenty thousand a draw, the odds are still seventy-two to one against you.

>

By some lucky twist of fate, the draw that night was one of those guaranteed bonanzas that come up every now and then.

"It's an omen!" hissed Daniel. "We're going to win! We're going to win the big one!" Both he and my mother seemed to have shelved their reservations about theft. They had evidently decided that we would split the millions between the three of us. A melange of colored balls swirled obediently inside the glass bubble. A central column popped up and the first ball was on its way. It settled in the chute.

Forty-eight.

We all screamed and bounced and grabbed each other's arms as if we had already won.

"Keep calm!" warned Daniel. "There are still five numbers to go..."

Forty-six. Twelve.

More bouncing. More screaming.

"Keep calm!" repeated Daniel. "I've had three numbers before. Along with fifty thousand other ticket holders. You win about twenty rand!" But even he nearly expired when we got the fourth one too. I was ready to fire an impatient bullet at the screen by the time the final balls settled in their slots.

Twenty five and nine. We stared disbelievingly at the screen.

"But those are the wrong numbers," said my mother stupidly, sounding like an escaped moron.

I slumped, defeated, in my chair. As if I'd been savaged by a pit-bull. There were over seven hundred tickets with four correct numbers that day. The stats were right. No one ever really wins the Lotto. Our prize came to less than a trolley-load of groceries. We shrugged resignedly and carried on with our lives.

Secretly, I was quite relieved. I wouldn't have been able to squander twenty million without a pang of guilt. It's a bit late to be plagued by moral scruples, considering the pile of stolen goods already piled up in my secret drawer, but I'd never pilfered cash before. Nothing I stole was random. I could have fobbed off a psychologist with an emotional reason to explain each individual theft. I could even have dug up an explanation about what motivated me to swap the Lotto tickets, but the fact that my delinquency paid out in cash somehow made it more reprehensible.

I couldn't bring myself to spend the money I won on my stolen Lotto ticket. I took the trouble to visit the bank and open an additional account. I called it 'Lotto' and made the opening deposit with my paltry winnings. I forgot all about it once I left the bank, so it sat in the vault, gathering interest.

Maybe I could say that it grew like a cancer, considering how I eventually spent the money.

TWO

I can give the date when I felt the first flutter of anxiety. 22 January 2007. It was noted in my diary because my mother was lecturing on the role of conflict in her novels at a creative writing course offered as part of the Summer School programme at UCT.

There were two schools of thought about creative writing in Cape Town at the time. My mother was fiercely opposed to the one which advocated writing down your thoughts in whatever jumble they occurred to you.

"You should go to a therapist rather than a publisher if you need some cathartic cleansing," she maintained emphatically. "It may make you feel better to put your anger down on paper but publishers don't give a damn if you feel better or not. They're only interested in something they can sell. And you can't sell jumbled thoughts. Only your therapist cares about the issues that come up in your dreams."

She was a great believer in structure. There was nothing autobiographical about her novels. They would certainly be filed under fiction. Her own life might have been unravelling in fifteen different directions at the same time, but her editor told me that she seldom found a typing error in my mother's manuscripts. Or even a misplaced comma. My mother preached the gospel of revision. She might have a sudden flood of inspiration, but she'd go back and check out what she'd written, almost immediately. She was like Sherlock Holmes, always on the alert for inconsistencies in her characters' behaviour or time scale.

I wish I'd been more like Sherlock Holmes in detecting clues on her inconsistencies. I still feel careless about my inattention, even though there's nothing I could have done to deflect the outcome.

She was sitting at the dining room table when I dropped in. There was the usual sea of papers in front of her, but she was staring at a letter in her hands.

"You look a bit bemused," I said as I made my way past the table, en route to search for a tea bag in the kitchen which was starting to become as hard to navigate as the dining room table. She appeared to have abandoned the systematic storage of groceries. Misplacing things in inappropriate places is another clue that Sherlock would have pounced on if he'd been on the case.

"What speed were you going this time?" I asked. I knew that bemused look. It was usually related to traffic fines. She always claimed she was innocent.

"It's from Ron," she said. "Confirmation for the creative writing course at Summer School. I don't remember agreeing to speak."

My mother was often asked to speak at writing courses, not only because she'd had five novels published. She was as fluent verbally as she was on paper. She'd had a lifetime of missed deadlines and impromptu deliveries, so she handled unexpected questions with aplomb. Her skills came in useful when the students handed their own work in for discussion. She could always pinpoint a weakness, make suggestions about possible alternatives. She had presence. She would have been a wonderful teacher, but I'm sure they would have fired her when they got to know her better. She would have lost her mark book and pitched up late for lessons every day.

My mother has made the pilgrimage to UCT for Summer School every January for as long as I can remember. She always found a course related to something she was researching at the moment or that she thought might be useful at some point in the distant future. There's a special Summer School shelf in the dining room, weighed down with notes she had taken on various topics.

"But that's great!" I said. "Congratulations! Your fame is definitely spreading!"

She shrugged her shoulders. I could feel her anxiety when I finally located the tea bags in the fridge and sat down beside her at the table with two hot cups steaming reassuringly. There's something comforting about a cup of tea, but it didn't seem to have the desired effect.

"They'll love you," I told her. "You're a million times better than that guy who spoke at the French cuisine lecture you dragged me to last year. He stood behind the lectern and read out his notes. I might as well have been listening to the janitor. I'd much rather listen to you than listen to him, even if he is a world authority."

"I don't remember agreeing to speak," she said again. That seemed to worry her more than the speech itself. She also knew she couldn't just read out her notes at the creative writing class because it's a workshop. Entry is restricted to twenty people. In some ways, it's more demanding than speaking to a crowd of strangers in a lecture theatre. The courses are bloody expensive, so the people who come aren't doing so merely on a whim. They expect to make some progress. She handed me the program. The course was divided into sections on beginnings, characters, dialogue and conflict. She was listed as the keynote speaker for the session on conflict.

"I don't remember agreeing to speak," she said again. She was beginning to annoy me.

"You'll be fine," I said, sipping my tea and shelving the subject altogether.

>

I took time off work to take her to Summer School myself. She needed help because her car was at the panel beater being repaired. She'd misjudged the distance between the car and the gate and gouged out a major scar along the side panel.

"For God's sake," I yelled. "Why didn't you stop when

you hit it? You must have reversed back and forwards about fifteen times to do this much damage!"

My mother had a long history of car confrontations. This was just another incident in a long string of them. Since the car was still in the throes of being beaten back into shape, she arranged with the convener for me to sit in on the session, ready to drive her home afterwards.

She delivered her speech with her usual style. All her novels are set in South Africa. She traced the way the conflicts she raised in each one reflected the political changes taking place at the time. It wasn't a big lecture hall, so it felt more as if we were out to dinner than at a public lecture. Since the people who came to the course were expected to be familiar with the writing of the speakers, she was able to refer to each of her novels to illustrate the points she was making. God knows how she remembers them in so much detail. I couldn't remember even their titles if I had to name them in a quiz.

I was the only one in the class who wasn't writing furiously. It seems that my mother isn't the only compulsive notetaker at Summer School. I can't imagine why anyone might want to make notes on someone else's novel. English literature was a mystery to me in high school.

My attention really started to wander when the students began to chip in with questions about her speech. A woman with a strident voice was holding the floor and had just asked my mother a daunting question about the conflicts facing South African women in her novels. She looked like one of those rabid feminist types. No doubt she'd already burned her bra. You often get people like her who use question time to make a speech of their own. I didn't have a clue what she was talking about.

I became aware that my mother didn't seem to know what she was talking about either.

The strident woman finally finished talking. Her question hung unanswered in the air. The room was very quiet now that the strident voice had faded. I thought initially that my mother was just gathering her thoughts. She often took her time to answer a question. It was one of her skills. She had the knack of making people feel that their question had raised an interesting aspect of the subject under discussion. But this silence was longer than usual. It became uncomfortable. I was aware of people fidgeting in their chairs, exchanging glances. My mother just sat there, smoothing out a wrinkle on the cuff of her shirt.

I didn't know what to do. I could see the convener didn't either.

"Chloe?" he asked eventually. "Any thoughts on Jenny's question?"

My mother looked at him blankly.

"What was the question?" she asked.

Even strident Jenny looked disconcerted. She rephrased her question, but my mother still didn't seem to hear it. Her attention was completely focused on the wrinkle on her cuff. The silence stretched and fingered all corners of the room. The class had started pretending not to look at my mother. It was embarrassing. The convener obviously decided to cut his losses and run. He said that he would move on to the workshop section of the morning where the students would have to write a piece of their own, revolving around conflict. I was aware of both relief and curiosity hanging in the air as he thanked my mother for her contribution. She just sat there. I got up and took her arm and led her out of the lecture hall. It seems amazing in retrospect, but even then I didn't register what was happening.

My mother once made us all laugh at a dinner party when she read sections from a hilarious book she'd just bought. It's called *Mortification* or something like that. It's a series of pieces written by names as famous as Margaret Atwood and Margaret Drabble. A whole lot of them have won the Booker Prize on some occasion. They describe scenes where they have been utterly humiliated in public. The debacles range from forgetting the titles of their books, becoming totally incoherent in an interview, or having to address an empty hall at a book launch. I expected my mother's account of her experience at Summer School to fall into that category. I was even looking forward to it.

"Christ!" I thought she'd say, grabbing my arm and burying her head on my shoulder. "I felt like Lawrence of Arabia confronted by the vastness of the Sahara desert. Miles and miles of sand and not a single word on the horizon! That woman's voice alone was enough to render even a Shakespearean actor speechless!" I'd shriek with sympathetic laugher, and we'd stop off at the wine-bar on the way home for a recuperative drink or two. By the time we got home, the story would have grown into a twenty-minute anecdote to get the whole table laughing at her next dinner party.

But that didn't happen. She didn't mention the incident at all. It was as if she hadn't noticed it had taken place. She chatted cheerfully about the lecture and the convener and Summer School in general, but she seemed completely unaware that the morning had ended in such a disastrous manner. I was frightened by the time that I dropped her off because my own memory was functioning more efficiently than usual.

I remembered Iris Murdoch.

I have a copy of *Iris* in my DVD collection. I bought it because she reminded me of my mother. I'm not insane enough to imagine that my mother's writing is in her class. Iris Murdoch was a Dame of the British Empire and lectured in philosophy at Oxford. My mother made a niche for herself in the small field of local stories around the struggle to end apartheid. They may not be comparable in literary terms, but when I watched the movie about Iris, something about her early zest for life and disregard for public opinion struck a chord. Even her old, bumbling husband seemed familiar. I know he's a university professor, but he seemed like someone's grandfather. Most of my mother's lovers have been ageing academics. The last young god she slept with was my father. It was as if real sex ended when he died. His elderly successors always seemed more like a research project rather than a physical turn on. She was more interested in their conversation than their bodies.

I almost dreaded re-watching *Iris* when I pressed play the evening after the Summer School fiasco. I wasn't sure if I wanted to remember everything that movie tells us about Alzheimer's.

➤

THREE

I phoned my brother in Colorado when *Iris* ended.

He's been with his current girlfriend for longer than usual. She's a Native American, but Karl accused us of racism when my mother and I started to refer to her as Pocahontas. Race appears to be as sensitive an issue in North America as it is in South Africa. We've never met her, but she's got a master's degree in Environmental Science which puts her multiple rungs above my brother who barely scraped Matric — the only skill mentioned in his CV would be pizza delivery. Her luckless parents must have been hysterical when their brainy daughter hooked up with Karl. He looks as if he's stepped out of an advert for Camel Man which probably explains it. All my friends have been in love with Karl at some stage.

He and Pocahontas have gone back to nature in a commune where they milk cows and weave mats. Unfortunately, it's in a different time zone to Cape Town —

he was pretty unreceptive when I woke him up at two in the morning to tell him that our mother had Alzheimer's.

"For Christ's sake, Hannah," he snarled. "You're such a prima donna. She's had a memory crisis her entire life. She probably forgot to wake up for her midnight feed when she was still in her cradle. Why phone me in the middle of the night to tell me something we've been aware of for decades?"

"But this is different," I protested. "Yesterday was really weird." I told him about the question time fiasco.

"Oh please," he said scornfully. "That doesn't sound so catastrophic. Don't be such a drama queen. Anyone can have a blank. I'm quite likely to forget your name on occasion. You're making a fuss about nothing. You always manage to turn a tiny little mole hill into a major mountain. Stop worrying and let me get some sleep."

I tried to stop worrying when he put the phone down. I have a tendency to make issues where none exist, but I couldn't wipe it out of my mind entirely. Too many incidents in Iris Murdoch's life rang bells for me about my mother's behaviour. I'd dismissed it as eccentricity, but the movie made me look at the situation through Iris-eyes.

➤

My Iris-eyes kept me awake that night, even though the room was dark and quiet, my pillow and duvet reassuringly familiar. My mind was a muddle of memories: as if I was scared to let myself forget. Disjointed thoughts jostled for position, elbowed their unrelated way forward, out of sequence. They centered round my mother.

My newly-vulnerable mother. One of my mothers. It felt like a jigsaw, but the pieces were too jumbled to make a pattern which I could recognize. Maybe it was more like dominos with their landmark chain reaction.

The trigger for the domino effect that night was my mother's lecture. I remembered feeling proud when she was introduced. Chloe Cartwright, a well-known name in literary and journalistic circles, the convenor told us. A political activist who'd written a column for the *Mail&Guardian* for decades. Some of her columns were published in the *Guardian* in London, once she'd established herself as a struggle author. Penguin had published five of her novels. Karl and I called them the *Not-So-Famous-Five*. No one ever seems to buy a copy, judging by the royalties.

It struck me as I lay sleeplessly under my duvet that my mother's occupation had never seemed as clear cut to me as the convenor made it sound at Summer School. I certainly couldn't say she was a housewife. My father died when I was a baby, so she was never a wife of any sort, in my experience. She certainly wasn't celibate, but she never committed herself to one man after my father's death. Julia thought it was romantic – her mother agreed with her. Julia and I sometimes got our mothers mixed up. I think she may have loved mine more than I did, but she didn't have to live with her.

My mother kept irregular hours as a writer. None of the multiple achievements trotted out in the Summer School introduction ever led to solvency. Teachers and nurses are notoriously badly paid in South Africa, but I think they're better off than freelance journalists. At least they get paid every month. Karl and I used to complain that no teenager could survive on the pocket money she doled out to us on an intermittent basis. She fobbed us off with her trademark excuse. "Authors can't make money in a country where only about ten per cent of the population ever buys a book," she told us. We kept praying that some foreign Penguin would snap up the rights for one of the *Not-So-Famous-Five*, but it never happened.

Karl and I were used to a precarious existence. Sometimes a flurry of articles was accepted in the same month and hallelujah, we were solvent! If we'd had an accountant as our father, he'd have stored up the surplus in the bank to cover the ballet fees in the lean times that inevitably lay ahead, but my mother never did that.

"Put on your glad rags, my darlings!" she'd yell whenever she heard that one of her features had been accepted. "We're dining out!" We never went to reasonably priced family restaurants. I developed a taste for exotic food long before I met Daniel.

➤

Karl and I once watched a re-run of a Joan Crawford movie on some late-night TV channel after we were supposed to be in bed. Bedtime was a detail my mother tended to overlook when she was busy on a story. *Mommie Dearest* is rated one of the campest movies of all time. It won Worst Picture and Worst Actress and a host of other Worsts the year it was released.

Karl and I have always said that that our mother could have walked off with a few accolades in the Worst Mother category. She would be unmatched as Worst Provider of a Wholesome Family Meal. Or Homework Supervision. Or Attendance at Parents' Night.

We didn't complain about neglect to the school counselor. My mother's maternal skills were perfect from our point of view. We were never anxious about the arrival of our school reports, although we would have had good reason to be worried in a more normal home environment. We were as thick as planks and did no work at all which is not a winning combination in the classroom. We knew she'd laugh derisively when she read the list of criticism and complaints from our luckless teachers.

"What the fuck do they know?" I remember her saying as she crumpled the report into a ball and threw it in one of our directions. Our fielding skills were better than our marks – we would catch it and throw it back to her or to each other and then into the bin. There were no family archives of school reports in our house.

Unlike most parents on the planet, my mother was more interested in movies than in formal education. She was prone to getting up just in time to make it to the morning show. Karl and I went with her on school holidays. We occasionally went with her during the term as well, when the alarm failed to get us up in time to make school assembly. We once had the misfortune to bump into Mrs. Holmes, my class teacher, as we were gobbling down our popcorn in the queue.

"They're feeling sick," said my mother blandly, looking Mrs. Holmes brazenly in the eye. "I'm trying to cheer them up. You know how they hate to miss a day at school."

Mrs. Holmes was completely wrong-footed. She just nodded and hurried on her way. She must have heard us laughing as she turned the corner. I bet she had a few things to say in the staffroom when she got back, but we heard no more about it. Maybe Mrs Holmes was bunking herself.

➤

I was embarrassed to have a mad mother when I was at school. I adopted alternative mothers like other kids collect stamps.

Julia's mother was my favorite. I wished I could wave a wand and install her at the head of our dining room table in place of my own mother. Not that my mother ever presided at the head of our dining room table in the way one might expect from the family matriarch. We never used our dining room table in the context of a family meal. It was home to my mother's computer. It was entirely buried under books and scraps of scrawled notes or newspapers articles on whatever feature she was currently researching. There would have been no use for a dining room table, even if a sudden avalanche of paper suddenly fell off it and cleared the way for a chicken casserole. My mother used to write the occasional article on cooking, but that was about as close as she got to a casserole. God knows why Karl and I didn't grow up with rickets and rotting teeth.

"What's for supper?" we'd whine in a plaintive way.

"Have a piece of bread!" she'd cry feverishly as she rushed to meet her deadline. A failure to reach deadlines was the trademark of my mother's freelance career. It was even worse when she was working on a book. She would shut herself in her room and cast out the occasional fifty rand note as a gesture, en route to relieving the famine which usually prevailed in our fridge. We were like orphans in the storm as we made our way down to the corner café for chicken and chips. Our plight was unfortunately never picked up by a social worker. I blame our departed father for his macho genes. Karl and I were both the biggest kids in our respective classes. Malnutrition wasn't a word that came to mind when you looked at the pair of us.

Julia was like a wraith in comparison, despite the wholesome meals she was served on a daily basis. I loved the order and formality that was part of the package that came with spending the night at Julia's. Supper was served at six. The table was laid and everyone sat down in a specific chair. Everyone was wearing clothes. No one slouched around in boxer shorts like Karl. We all bowed our heads while Julia's dad said grace and then Julia's mom brought in the food. I particularly liked her roast potatoes with their crisp brown crust and their soft, fluffy insides.

"I spend a fortune on imported olive oil," explained Julia's mom.

That's another reason why I loved her. She always answered my questions as if they'd been posed by a proper person, as opposed to some scruffy friend that her daughter had picked up at school. I was always interested in cooking, even as a child. I used to waste my time by taking home the formula for some delicious dish that Julia's mom had conjured up in her orderly and well-stocked kitchen. My mother's efforts at roast potatoes could easily have been loaded into a handgun. A few extra bullets might come in handy, considering Cape Town's crime rate...

Strangely enough, Julia also loved staying the night with me. We never had enough money to go to the movies so having friends to stay was our version of a treat.

"Of course you don't have to go to bed, my little treasures!" my mother would assure us when Karl and his friends complained that Julia and I were following them around and getting in the way. Julia was besotted with Karl. She stuck to him like glue.

"Come on, Karl," my mother would urge. "Show some initiative. Divert them. Set up a treasure hunt or something." My mother was always pretty keen to have us diverted.

"I refuse to set up another bloody treasure hunt," moaned my luckless elder brother. "Send them to bed, like normal children."

"Come on, Karl," she repeated, with her eye on her computer and her deadline. "Ten rand for a treasure hunt."

"I'll do it for fifty," offered Karl who had a teenage tendency to live beyond his budget. He was always open to a bribe.

"Make it twenty, and it's a deal!" yelled Julia, eager to take part in the informal auctions that were part of the Cartwright family ethos.

"It's on!" cried my mother. "And you're the treasure!" she cried, sweeping little Julia off her feet. "Quick, Karl! Hide the treasure before Hannah sees you!" She'd throw Julia over to Karl who whirled her round like a flying saucer before burying her under a pile of cushions on the couch. Julia shrieked with laughter! No one threw her around in her house! Especially not at eleven at night! Sleepovers at the Cartwrights were sought after invitations when I was at primary school. Julia and I shuttled back and forth between each other's houses on such a regular basis that it sometimes seemed we were all part of the same family.

"Your mom's so cool!" Julia would sigh wistfully, after another late night of coffee and conversation around the dining room table with my mother. "She's more like a friend than a mom."

But I didn't want my mother to be my friend. Julia was my best friend so I didn't need another one. What I wanted was a mother. A motherly mother. One who would look after me.

I had to stop my retrospective brooding on the nature of mothers because it was morning. I didn't tell Daniel about my concerns, but as soon as he left for work, I made my way to my mother's house on Pepper Street. I needed to inspect the situation through my Iris-eyes. I was afraid the tables might have turned.

Maybe it was time for me to start looking after her?

FOUR

It's ironic that the state of my mother's house was the first thing I registered when I paid attention to her world from my new perspective. She would never have walked off with an award for Housekeeper of the Year. Domesticity had never been high on her agenda. She would rather read us a bedtime story than make the bed. Our dining room table hadn't seen the light of day for years. It had been littered with piles of paper for as long as I remember, but I noticed a subtle difference when I dropped in after my sleepless night.

In the past, the piles had always had some semblance of order. The book-review file was always perched in the left-hand corner beside the notes from the most recent Summer School lectures. They were promoted to the shelf beside the table when she'd finished working on them. Notes relating to the current novel or magazine feature were always given pride of place to the left of the computer keyboard. They were surrounded by a posse of smaller piles which were related to the main feature in some way. To an outsider, it must have looked like a total shambles, but I knew the code she used to decipher a route around the maze. Structure is a strength in my mother's novels, and it was reflected in the seeming chaos that she worked with every day.

She wasn't at her desk when I arrived. I cast my new, discerning Iris-eyes around the table. I felt a stab of anxiety as I made a cursory sift through her work-in-progress pile beside the keyboard. There was nothing wrong with the pages I glanced through, other than the order. But that didn't worry me. She might have had some particular reason for printing out those pages in that order. The aspect that jarred was that the pages were interspersed with notes from the Summer School lecture she'd attended earlier that month.

It was about cultural stereotypes of Japanese women as depicted in prints and paintings from as early as the sixth century. She went to the lecture to get background for a freelance feature she was doing on Japanese décor for a design magazine. She talked a lot about her plots while she was writing so I knew her new novel was about a woman in Cape Town trying to come to terms with the emigration of her children. It had nothing to do with geishas in Japan. The topics are totally unrelated. She would never have had those notes in the same pile in the old days.

She had always been meticulous about the chaos that

reigned on her desk, but now there seemed to be a new dimension to the disorder. Was it a reflection of what was happening inside her brain?

>

I peered into the kitchen to see if my mother was there. I walked over and opened the fridge, looking for clues. It was as if I had turned into Sherlock Holmes. The characteristic feature of the kitchen of my childhood was an empty fridge. No milk. No eggs. Definitely not a grilled chicken, waiting to be dismembered and gobbled down as a lunch-time snack. God knows why my mother was so fat because I never remember her eating anything. Maybe it's genetic. I'm also a size to be reckoned with. Alzheimer's too is genetic and perhaps the cold clutch of fear as I registered the contents of the fridge that morning was partly for my own future.

It wasn't empty now. There was milk and cheese. Two cartons of yogurt and a bowl of salad. But all of them were past their sell-by date. It was if she'd forgotten they were there. The milk was sour. Both yogurt cartons were empty. Why would she put empty yogurt containers back in the fridge? Even a starving mouse would have turned its nose up at the cheese and there can be few things less appetizing than a limp lettuce and an ageing tomato. It looked as if my mother had been away on a six-month holiday.

My Iris-eyes took in the rest of the kitchen. Unwashed cups and plates piled up in the sink. Breadcrumbs beside an open loaf of bread. A can of baked beans, half full. The stove top looked as if it had been in contact with a volcano. There'd obviously been a crisis involving a bolognaise sauce. There were old newspapers and dusty glasses. I was appalled. Our kitchen had been untidy in the past, but when did it become so dirty? I don't know why it had taken me so long to register what was happening.

>

I found my mother sitting in the lounge, looking at the window rather than out of it. Well, that's how it seemed to me. She didn't seem to be focused on anything. She was just sitting there, looking at the window.

"Hello there," I said. I bent over to kiss her.

"Hannah!" Her voice was as warm and welcoming as usual. I felt absurdly relieved. I'd almost been expecting her not to recognize me which was patently ridiculous. She couldn't have evolved into Iris Murdoch overnight. I'd heard her give a perfectly coherent lecture to twenty students, one day before. She'd given insights into her novels in the finest detail. It was crazy to write her off on the strength of a momentary lapse in concentration. The disorder on the dining room table and in the kitchen could have a perfectly logical explanation. I pulled myself together and we carried on with a normal conversation. The visit passed without further incident, but I couldn't quite dispel a sense of unease as I drove home afterwards.

I'd felt a flash of recognition when I saw her sitting looking at the window. Her face had the same blankness that Judy Dench captured so poignantly in her portrayal of Iris Murdoch. I've since learned that the lion-face is a clinical description of Alzheimer's patients. Their features settle into a broad, expressionless mask which Murdoch's husband describes in his account of his wife's illness. A leonine passivity, he calls it, as if the patient has become a sculpture or a mask, lacking any animation or vitality. Neither tragic nor comic.

The face of an Alzheimer sufferer is indicative only of absence.

➤

Karl was less hostile when I phoned to tell him about the house inspection because I timed the call to coincide with daylight in his time-zone.

"But how can the house have got so dirty?" was his first question. "What's happened to Happy Housewives or whatever they're called?"

He meant Marvellous Maids. It's a house cleaning service that my mother used on a weekly basis. When Karl and I were kids, my mother had a full-time maid in true South African tradition. Miriam had been one of my multiple mothers. She was at home a lot more than my mother and played a key role in ensuring that the house didn't descend into a state of squalor. Unfortunately, her duties didn't extend as far as cooking, but cleaning and ironing were invaluable to the functioning of the house.

But times change. Miriam was even older than my mother and chose to go back to her family in the Transkei when she developed arthritis in her hands and back. My mother felt ethically obliged to pay her a decent pension, after all her years as the faithful family retainer which made a dent in her budget that she could ill afford. There are pension schemes which she could have paid into for Miriam's retirement, but my mother wasn't noted for planning ahead. Family retainers in South Africa always come with a half a dozen dependants who also make regular dents in the family budget. Someone was always dying or getting married or needing school fees. Karl and I had both left home by the time Miriam rode off into the sunset. My mother decided that a Marvellous Maid once a week would be a better deal for her, now that she was on her own in the house. You didn't get the same Marvel every week so she wouldn't become part of the family like Miriam.

It looked as if phoning Marvellous Maids was another thing my mother had forgotten to do that month.

"It is worrying," conceded Karl when I explained. "But how are you planning to get her to a doctor? You can hardly look her in the eye and mention Alzheimer's."

Karl had isolated the problem in an instant. I'd grown up certain that my big brother knew all the answers, but I learned as we got older that he knew all the questions too. How does one introduce the A word into a conversation with someone still functional enough to know everything that Alzheimer's implies about her future?

Especially if she's only fifty-nine.

➤

It was after midnight when I got the phone-call from the Engen garage in Khayelitsha. Daniel was away, and I was dozing in a muggy pre-sleep stage after another night of concern about my mother's health. I jolted to attention when the phone jarred on the table beside the bed. I threw off the duvet and leapt across the space between the bed and the table like an Olympic athlete in the long jump pit. I always assume that someone's dead when the phone rings in the middle of the night.

"Hello?" Anxiety coursed through me.

I heard a black man's voice at the other end of the line. Not Daniel. Not a voice I recognized. Let's face it. Calls after midnight are never good news unless your daughter's pregnant. I didn't have a pregnant daughter so this was definitely bad news.

"Is that Hannah?" asked my mystery caller which made it even more ominous. One holds onto the hope that maybe it's a wrong number.

"My mother." It was more of a statement than a question. My mind continued down a mangled route that led to blood and dented metal. "Is she all right?" I'm sure he could hardly hear me. I'd lowered my voice to an inexplicable whisper, as if I was afraid I might wake her up if spoke too loudly.

"Yes, yes," said the voice. It was deep reassuring voice with a hint of laughter in its texture. "She is fine. But she is lost."

"Lost?" I sounded like some kind of low-grade parrot.

He said she'd taken a wrong turn on the way home from the airport. She was at the Engen garage in Khayelitsha.

"Khayelitsha?" I howled disbelievingly, turning my

voice up to a full-blown screech. The Khayelitsha off-ramp is halfway to Somerset West. It's in the opposite direction from Cape Town. "Let me speak to her."

But he didn't want to let me speak to her. Or maybe she didn't want to speak to me. Maybe she was shaking her head when he offered her the phone. I was stuck with the petrol attendant.

"Can't you give her directions?" I pleaded.

No, said the reassuring voice, he didn't want to give her directions. She seemed muddled. He thought I should come and fetch her.

"Christ," I muttered, as I pulled on a tracksuit over my pajamas. "Bloody woman!" She's going into a home tomorrow, I decided. I drove aggressively up the empty freeway, my hands clenched around the wheel. I had an early appointment tomorrow, and I hadn't washed my hair. The last thing I bloody needed was a midnight trip to Khayelitsha.

Khayelitsha is a suburb of Cape Town, just like the Bo-Kaap. Neither have English names, but the Bo-Kaap sounds a lot safer than Khayelitsha if you've grown up in South Africa. Residential apartheid has blurred boundaries now, but the poverty divide is still firmly in place, despite the best intentions of the ANC. I knew my way to Khayelitsha a lot better than most white people in Cape Town, but I still wasn't keen to drive there in the middle of the night. A taxi load of gangsters seemed much more likely to pull up at a garage in Khayelitsha than outside Daniel's house in Gardens.

The Engen garage was rather an anti-climax when I finally arrived. It looked completely free of criminals and hostile vagrants, who I imagined might have been eager to rob me if they'd been there. I screeched to a halt beside my mother's snappy little Hyundai, safely parked outside the garage shop. She wasn't waiting anxiously up on the verge, pacing up and down. I rushed into the shop. She was sitting on a chair with her notebook up on the counter. She appeared to be interviewing the petrol attendant.

"Mom!" I exploded, more loudly than I intended. "Are you all right? What happened?"

"Oh, hello, Hannah," she said vaguely, as if it wasn't the middle of the night, on the fringe of what I still suspected was a ghetto of squatters, poised and waiting to steal our cars and snatch our credit cards. "Thanks for coming, darling. I got a bit muddled with the off-ramps on the way from dropping Jenny at the airport. You know it's a bit confusing in the dark."

"Confusing?" I yelled in disbelief. "It's in the opposite fucking direction!"

I think that was the closest I came to getting mugged on my midnight excursion. The petrol attendant looked very disapproving. My mother patted him reassuringly on the arm.

"Hannah always overreacts!" she told him. "You know how impatient daughters are with their mothers! I was just the same with my own mother! Guess it's payback time!" she chuckled, settling in her seat. The petrol attendant nodded knowingly and smiled. I'm surprised he didn't give a conspiratorial wink. I could see he liked her more than I did at that stage of the proceedings. My fear that she'd been raped and murdered began to evaporate. I was starting to wish she had been raped and murdered, to justify this crazy midnight journey across Cape Town in my pajamas. She seemed reluctant to end her interview with the petrol attendant who she introduced as Gideon.

"Have a cup of coffee," she said expansively. "I've nearly finished here!"

"You are finished here!" I snarled, sweeping up her notebook and snatching her pen out of her hand. "Get into the car and follow me home!"

I kept my eyes fastened in my rearview mirror all the way home. I was terrified she might head off to Paarl or Tableview, but we made it back to her garage without further incident. She didn't seem to register that anything untoward had happened as she hugged me on the doorstep and unlocked her already unlocked door. She didn't even thank me for saving the day. Or the middle of the night, as it happened to be.

I looked at my watch. It was half-past two. This was an impossible situation. My mother was as mad as a hatter on the one hand and completely functional on the other. Yet she'd never been completely functional, so it was simply a matter of degree in her case. She wrote an entertaining article on the midnight lifestyle of petrol attendants in all-night garages which was published in *The Weekender* a couple of weeks later. She even made me retrace our steps to the garage to take a photograph of Gideon who was delighted at the prospect of making the news.

But I couldn't write this off as a happily-ever-after-ending. South Africa has one of the highest crime rates in the world. It's not safe to be lost on the streets after midnight in either Khayelitsha – or Gardens, for that matter. My mother had turned in the opposite direction from Cape Town when she left the airport. She's done the airport run about a million times. It's almost as familiar as her own driveway.

There was something wrong. Not even my mother is as scatterbrained as that.

➤

FIVE

I was desperate to get back to bed after my unscheduled excursion to Khayelitsha, but I couldn't sleep when I switched off the light. I couldn't face another onslaught of jumbled memories. I decided on something constructive instead. I forced myself out of bed and made my bleary way to the computer.

I keyed in Alzheimer's.

I wasn't even certain how to spell it at that stage, but I obviously got it right because I got about five million hits. This was a bit overwhelming for an inexperienced researcher like me. *Gird your loins,* I told myself. I started scrolling down. It was uniformly depressing.

The first site claimed that there would be two billion people over sixty in 2050, and ten per cent of them would have Alzheimer's. I get mixed up with the number of noughts in a billion – I can't remember how many millions that works out to, but I know it's more than a sizable crowd. It's a multitude. I'll be hitting eighty by then which means I'll probably be one of them. I wonder if anyone will tell me. Or even if I'd want to know.

That was my dilemma with my mother. Would she want to know what I suspected? It's not as if she was eighty-five years old. I'd never thought of her as elderly. I skimmed multiple pages on the symptoms of Alzheimer's. Memory loss, especially in the short term. Repetition. Losing everything in sight. Forgetting words as simple as a sugar bowl. It sounded dreadful, but the page on behavioural disturbances sounded even worse. Wandering. Agitation. Aggression. Paranoia. Delusions. Hallucinations.

My poor mother. Poor me. I felt guilty to be thinking of myself, but I knew I'd have to look after her. Karl wouldn't be much help with the Atlantic Ocean and North America in the way. It was inconceivable to imagine her in an old age home. I scrolled on.

There were lots of complicated explanations about what was happening in her brain. Plaques and tangles. Something called the hippocampus seemed to be a central player. It was beyond me. I just scrolled on regardless. I was looking for pages which listed cures, but there weren't any of those. I found a few drugs which could possibly slow the process down – with side-effects, of course. I didn't find a single one that would reverse the process or stop it from happening altogether. I'd printed out sheets of information by the time I decided I had more information than I could handle. My bedroom was starting to look like my mother's dining room table.

But I was too scared to give the information to my mother. I screwed it all up into a ball and threw it in the dustbin. I would rather have burned it, but there was so much paper that I was afraid it might cause a conflagration. I had to somehow get her to the doctor. He could fill her in on the details. Maybe there was some other explanation. Maybe I was wrong. Why upset her with an unqualified diagnosis?

I got back into bed. This time I did fall asleep.

>

I told my mother I wanted to make an appointment for her to see the doctor.

"You've been looking a bit peaky," I told her in a nonchalant kind of way. "I know you'll never get round to doing it yourself, and I think we need to see him for a check-up."

She sounded anything but muddled when she pounced upon my inoffensive little pronoun. "*We* need to see a doctor?" she asked. "Since when did going to the doctor become a joint effort? Are we going to strip together and have a simultaneous pap smear?"

I knew I couldn't beat around the bush forever, but I still tried to linger in the undergrowth.

"Well," I said reluctantly. She knew I was evading the issue. "Well...actually, Mom, I was a bit thrown by your Khayelitsha excursion. And a few other things, here and there. This and that. I'm a bit worried about your memory. I thought it might be helpful if I came along as well." I didn't sound as if I'd be much help. It sounded as if my own memory was in deep trouble.

"My memory?" said my mother. A cunning look crossed her face. She looked a bit like Shylock with a devious plan in mind. "You think I've lost it, don't you? You think I've got...um...um...whatitsname disease."

There was an awkward pause. Then she shrieked with laughter.

"Got you there!" she laughed. "I know all about Alzheimer's, and...I can assure you, I haven't got it!" She told me she'd also done some reading. That worried me. Her memory must have been worrying her too. "It's perfectly normal to lose your keys at my age," she assured me. "Don't worry about Khayelitsha. Anyone can get disorientated in the dark."

"But you know the airport road so well. You can almost drive it in your sleep. And the last time you lost your keys, I found them in the bath. That's more than being forgetful. That's peculiar."

"Oh nonsense, Hannah! I've always been a mad old bat! Don't suddenly make my personality into a symptom. We've muddled along all our lives and look how successful we've been."

That sentence alone was enough to have her committed on the spot. She'd written five failed novels. I'd barely managed to scrape through Matric, and Karl was weaving raffia mats in a commune in Colorado. None of us had managed to sustain a long-term relationship. Especially with a bank. Our family trio wasn't a very good advertisement for anyone advocating "muddling along" as a lifestyle.

>

I hadn't given genetics much thought until I started to worry about Alzheimer's. I never understood DNA and the double helix when they came up in biology at school. My life can't be described as cloistered so I do know that gene pools are pretty efficient when it comes to dishing out sex organs. They never tack on a willy by mistake when they're cooking up a little girl. You don't find many boys with ovaries and breasts but gene pools show less discretion when it comes to noses. I used to hold a grudge against my father over the nose issue until I realised that a nose is not the worst thing you can inherit. I try not to think about what is statistically likely to be part of my future from my mother's side of the family tree.

I'd been rather proud of my mother's story while I was growing up. My friends all had parents who were together or perhaps a parent in the throes of a messy divorce. I was the only one with a mother who had a romantic tragedy in her past. I trotted out the details whenever anyone asked me why she limped so badly. A rainy night. Poor visibility. The drunken driver. Screeching brakes. My dead father trapped behind the wheel. My mother's leg, twisted irretrievably. I was only a baby when it happened. I don't remember my father at all, but I've always been aware of his contribution to my gene pool because of the miscellany of photographs my mother has plastered on her walls. There was even one on the shelf facing the toilet. I couldn't take a pee without my father looking down on me.

He was a striking man. Even taller than my mother, with broad shoulders, powerful legs. He looked more like a film star than a human rights lawyer. I could understand why my mother struggled to replace him. The photo in the toilet is a tasteful sepia portrait which shows off his aquiline profile. This is where I could have done with a touch more discrimination from the gene pool that I share with Karl. It was far too even-handed. It seemed to give up on gender issues once my brother and I had been kitted out with everything we needed to propagate the species. We got an almost identical package after that.

Two hawk noses coming up. A couple of broad shoulders. Four powerful legs. I'm sure you get the picture. It's a pretty dismal one from a female point of view. I feel gloomy whenever I catch a glimpse of my profile in a mirror or a photo. A hawk-nose nose on Karl comes over as rugged. I'm surprised he was never snapped up for a Camel Man advert. A hawk-like nose on me is a different story altogether. All I'd ever get is a part in a pantomime. As a witch. Or maybe as a vulture in *The Lion King*. The same goes for powerful legs. Karl found them very handy on the right wing in first team rugby, but they did nothing to advance my ballet career. One look at my parents will tell you that no daughter of theirs would ever feature as Giselle.

➤

I'm sure I too would have played first team rugby if I hadn't been a girl. Julia and I filled in at the local park when Karl and his friends played touch rugby. I was bigger than most of the boys which made me valuable in any position. Julia opted for fly-half because she was fast and agile, but she was too small to make a major contribution. She was very pretty so no one minded. She was bruised and battered in the park, but she continued to turn up to play because she had a crush on Karl.

All my friends did. Girls adored my rugby-playing brother with his rakish good looks and his casual charm. My mother was also an ardent supporter of his rugby career which seemed completely out of character, considering her sparse attendance at school functions in general. I don't think she particularly liked rugby. I sometimes caught her scribbling notes instead of watching the game, but she pitched up to watch every match he played in, rain or shine. She even made a contribution to post-match teas, though she didn't go as far as baking the scones herself. We had a standing order at the Rose Cafe on Wale Street.

The staff at the Rose Cafe was another extension of my extended family. We'd lived in the same house in Pepper Street since my parents arrived from England in 1970, filled with determination to end apartheid.

The Bo-Kaap's become something of a tourist attraction in the new millennium, but Karl and I grew up as part of a small community of potters, artists and writers, living side by side with our Muslim neighbours – drifters and dreamers like my parents, fired up to deliver a brighter future. You don't see many children playing in

the streets today, but it was different while I was growing up. Most of our neighbours were Muslim. Islam's an
hospitable religion. There always seemed to be grannies
or aunties on the scene, ready to pick up stray toddlers if
an unexpected car turned down a neighbourhood street.
Someone was always at home. Parenting in the Bo-Kaap
seemed a shared responsibility.

This was fortuitous for our family. My parents had lived
in Pepper Street for just over a decade when my father
died. They came to South Africa as political activists in the
sixties after they became friendly with Thabo Mbeki at
Sussex University. He'd gone into exile – they had come
to the coal face to fight on his behalf.

My father set up a legal practice to try to free political detainees. He worked from home in a semi-detached
house like the one where my mother grew up in Brighton.
That's where the similarities stopped. Houses in Brighton
aren't painted orange or lime green. There's probably a
by-law against technicolored houses in England. The lime
green side of our house belonged to Fatima. I loved her
almost as much as I loved Julia's mother. She had even
more children. Karl and I were just two more, after my
father died. I was special because I was the only girl.

"Allah must have sent you," she used to tell me, as I sat
on her lap and listened to the story of how my mother fell
apart when my father died. "She wasn't strong enough to
get out of bed in the morning," Fatima used to say. "And
you were just a baby. You needed a mother and I needed
a little girl. I thank Allah every night for sending you to

Pepper Street." We sat on tall stools in her kitchen, our hands covered in biscuit dough for the cardamom biscuits Fatima supplied to the Rose Cafe.

"Ah, Hannah!" Hashim would say as I rushed in to collect our order before a first team match. "Where's Karl playing today?" I was delighted to be Karl Cartwright's little sister. He was essential to my self esteem. It gave me status to be related to a sporting legend.

"Karl says we should have won. Their try came off a forward pass," I'd tell them categorically as we ate our sandwiches and reflected on the weekend clash with Rondebosch or some other Southern Suburbs school. My acolytes sat around me in admiring circle. They shared their sandwiches with me on the days my mother got up too late to make them before I left for school. They hung on every word I had to say about rugby. I had as much prestige as if I was a commentator on the World Cup. This was the captain of the first team I was quoting, after all. I think they would have believed me if I'd told them that the captain of the rival team was an alien from Mars.

➤

My ballet career wasn't as auspicious as Karl's stint in first team rugby. My short-lived obsession was triggered by Julia's mother. Like my mother, she was no ordinary Cape Town housewife. She was a well-known name in her field. Completely unlike my mother, she logged out of the limelight when she fell pregnant. Julia's mom was pregnant for about a decade while giving birth to four children, allowing for a few gaps in between deliveries. Four pregnancies take more of a toll on your body than on your mind. Having children gave my mother fresh material to work with in her novels, but Julia's mom was a dancer. Pregnancy effectively ended her career.

She didn't look as if she'd had four children. She's tall and slender with an innate grace and poise. I worshipped her. I used to pray that I could rescue her from a fire. I considered starting one myself to give me the opportunity. I paged endlessly through the early pages of her scrapbook which were devoted to ballet, daring back to the start of her career with Capab. She was one of their principals by the time she left - there were dozens of programs featuring her name. Newspaper reviews and photos, where she starred as everything from a swan to a firebird. I loved her scrapbook.

My real mother also kept a scrapbook with photos and newspaper cuttings from the past, though it was less orderly than Julia's mother's. Coffee stains. Faded photos. Scribbled extracts from her books. Reviews of her books, from both local and English newspapers. Her scrapbook became even more meaningful to her when her past became clearer than her present. She nodded at photos of the semi-detached house in Brighton, where she grew up with older parents. I never met them, but she told me her father polished his ageing Rover every Saturday and they had pot roast on Sundays.

She became very repetitive with her stories of the past. She'd seen an escape route from English suburbia when Sussex University opened its doors, virtually next door to

Brighton. There were far fewer applications for Sussex than for the more venerable Oxbridge institutions, so she won a scholarship to study English and politics – exactly the sort of head-in-the-clouds subjects I'd have expected her to choose.

"There'll never be another decade like the sixties!" she'd declare each time she paged through posters of the Beatles and Harold Wilson. There was a faded photo of a group of friends, all cheering behind their placards.

"Look at us in 1964 – the first time Labour ever won in Brighton !" my mother reminisced. "We felt as if we'd played a part in history – all we ever did was hand out pamphlets at the robots!"

There were other photos of the same group of students, lined up behind various banners. They seemed to be anti-everything. The war in Vietnam. Nuclear power. UDI in Rhodesia. They were particularly anti-apartheid because of Thabo Mbeki. He stood out because he was the only black student at Sussex at the time. My mother often spoke at lectures about the night she and my father marched behind him, from Brighton to London, to hand in a petition at Downing Street about the death penalty.

I loved her scrapbook with its links to her past. My mother came to rely on it more and more as her illness progressed. She needed an activity to pass the time. She paged through her scrapbook almost every day because she forgot how to read.

> ✈

SIX

Julia's mother carted me along with Julia to ballet matinees once she realized that my own mother was unlikely to fill the cultural gap. I was an instant convert. I was enchanted by the music and the costumes and the grace of the dancers as they moved across the stage.

"I'm going to be a dancer," I said with resolution as we drove home after the first performance.

"Oh, Hannah," said Julia's mother ruefully. "It's such a hard career, my darling. Wouldn't you rather be a doctor and help sick people?"

"I'm not going to be a dancer or a doctor," said Julia firmly. "I'm going to be a pilot."

But there's no point in making plans. Your fate is coded into your gene pool. You can't hope to sidestep it and choose a future that's more to your liking. Julia was destined to dance from the moment she tried on the shoes at the Ballet Emporium. The future for both of us was written in stone on that expedition. Julia would go to the Royal School of Ballet in London. I'm lucky I didn't go to jail. If a judge ever asks me to tell the truth, the whole truth and nothing but the truth, I'd have to admit that it was the shopping expedition at the Ballet Emporium that triggered my career as a thief.

I was something of a child prodigy with regard to crime. I was still at primary school when I became aware of the easy answers it provides to a dilemma. If you want something, take it. And then you've got it. It's a very satisfying equation. It went so smoothly that I tried it again. And again. It turned into a habit. Shoplifting is a very popular career choice in urban South Africa today. Lots of people depend on it to earn their daily bread, but it was more of a hobby for me.

I don't remember feeling guilty. My light fingers didn't plague me and keep me from a good night's sleep. Psychologists are always keen to blame the parents, but neither of mine had a criminal orientation. My father died so young, he didn't have time to develop any deviant tendencies, and my mother was too inefficient to make a clean getaway. She would have been arrested on her first attempt. I didn't feel guilty about stealing because I felt that I deserved everything I stole. Or that my mother deserved it, in one case. I didn't see myself as a criminal. I must have been served a small helping of moral scruples in my genetic hand-out.

❧

I was desperate to start ballet lessons. I twirled optimistically in front of the full-length mirror in my mother's bedroom after the first matinee with Julia. I became a full-time twirler.

"Stop that, Hannah!" yelled either Karl or my mother as I twirled insanely past them on the way to supper or up the stairs to bed.

"Please...can I start ballet?" I begged and pleaded. "Please! Please!" I whined as I climbed into my mother's lap and wrapped my arms persuasively around her neck. "Karl goes to rugby! I never go to anything! Please can I go to ballet?"

This was quite a forceful argument. I was always being hauled out of bed on the weekend to go and watch Karl play rugby. My mother said I could go to ballet if Julia went too. It's a very time-consuming extramural and she knew it would never slot into her schedule.

Going to ballet with Julia was a bad decision from everyone's point of view. I could easily have been fobbed off with a few pliés in someone's garage down the street, but the situation changed once I'd persuaded Julia to enroll as well. Her mother was delighted when I prompted her daughter to swop rugby for ballet. She believed in good foundations and that meant a well-qualified teacher with a studio fitted out with a barre and wooden floors. Julia's family was in a different tax bracket than ours.

A court of law would never accuse Julia of being an accomplice in my shoplifting career, but she was directly responsible for the first two items I stole. I'd also lay some blame at my mother's door if a lawyer asked if there were any mitigating circumstances he could plead in my defense.

My mother was very irregular with pocket money handouts to Karl and me. It wasn't a problem for Karl because he'd already started delivering pizza while he was at high school. (We didn't know that it would be a career at that stage. He earned plenty of money in tips over the weekend. The Camel Man factor was useful, even as a teenager.)

Unfortunately, he never gave any of it to me. Both he and my mother regarded me as a child. They thought the only thing I needed was a school uniform, but no one does ballet on bare feet unless they live in a township. My needs stepped up a notch or two once I decided on a career in ballet, and my mother had to factor this into her budget. She didn't even come with me to buy my first pair of ballet shoes, although that seemed to be a mandatory task for all the other ballet mothers of my acquaintance. She just handed over the money to Julia's mom.

"Don't buy anything too expensive," she warned her. "You know what Hannah's like. This ballet fixation will probably last for two weeks, and then she'll be hounding me for ice skates!"

I thought we'd buy our ballet shoes at an ordinary shoe shop, but the Ballet Emporium in Long Street seemed more like Aladdin's cave when we got there. The costume section offered a rainbow range of tutus with tulle skirts and sequined tops, designed to delight any little princess who liked to dress up and transform herself into a fairy.

There were racks of ballet shoes and a comprehensive range of leotards and tights and leg warmers. There was a whole section of imported toys. Dolls in tutus. Ballet books and jigsaws. Ballet aprons and coloring books. There was a tiny music box with a dancer inside who spun around when you opened the lid.

Julia and I were in awe. We dropped our voices to a whisper as we prowled around and eavesdropped on her mother's conversation with the saleswoman who clearly wasn't a student earning money during the varsity vac. She sounded more like a ballet professor as she led us over to the racks of shoes. Julia's mother sounded a bit like a ballet professor herself as they discussed the merits and demerits of brand names like Bloch and Capezio. I hadn't heard of exchange rates at that stage, but I can imagine what they must have cost.

"I always preferred leather," said Julia's mom reflectively as she ran her hands knowledgeably over the shoe she picked up from the rack.

The saleswoman sounded delighted. She probably worked on a commission basis and scented money in the air. "They're certainly more durable than canvas. I always think they look more elegant," she answered. Elegance was hardly an issue considering that her customers were children, but Julia's mom didn't seem to find it irrelevant as she slipped a shoe onto her daughter's slender foot.

"It's too tight," moaned Julia with a marked lack of gratitude. Julia wasn't as interested in ballet as I was at that stage. The sales lady swept aside Julia's complaints about her snug-fitting Capezio shoe. "It must fit you as closely as a glove," she said as she made Julia balance on the balls of her feet while she felt around to see if her toes had room to move. I felt like the ugly sister as I took the other slipper out of the box and tried to cram my foot inside. The sales lady snatched it back disapprovingly. You'd think the shoe belonged to her rather than the Ballet Emporium.

"You're stretching it!" she snarled. "My darling," she added as an afterthought. Perhaps snarling at customers was against company policy at the Ballet Emporium.

"Let's see what you've got in canvas for Hannah," said Julia's mom when she saw the price tag on the leather pair she'd chosen for her daughter. "A local make is fine," she added. It couldn't have been an easy situation for her. She could hardly go home to my mother and ask for extra money.

"I want the same ones as Julia," I said despairingly while I tried on the canvas pair the saleswoman picked off the shelf. Being absolutely identical to one's best friend is a major issue when you're in primary school.

"These ones are just as nice, darling," said Julia's mom reassuringly. "Look. They've even got elastics to keep them on your feet. Your mom won't have to sew them on herself. And they can just be put in the washing machine." She must have picked up that my mother's housekeeping skills were as deficient as the family budget. The canvas shoes were perfect, of course. I wouldn't have known the difference if I hadn't watched Julia pivoting around the shop in her leather ones. It was the same with the leotards. Julia got a Doveskin leotard with a camisole top. I got a no-name brand with a plain round neck. And Julia also got a pink ballet bag with stars and moons printed on it.

I was very unhappy with my lot. That's when I first considered shoplifting as a way around the problem.

➤

There are a number of websites devoted to shoplifting. They say it's a psychological issue – people struggling with inner conflicts. But they say that about any deviant behaviour. You can get away with murder on much the same grounds.

Google wasn't around when I launched my shoplifting career, but I checked out shoplifting in retrospect, once the web became a way of life. I don't think I've ever been a kleptomaniac. A fringe kleptomaniac, perhaps. A real kleptomaniac can't stop herself from stealing, but my thefts were more in the category of fairy tales. I hoped that each would translate a fantasy into reality. Shoplifting was my version of a magic spell. The spells never worked, but that didn't stop me from hoping. Or from trying again.

My first theft is embedded in my mind in three dimensions. I remember how quiet it was. We were the only people in the shop. Julia was prancing around in the tutu section, holding tulle confections up against herself in front of the mirror. Her mother and the sales lady were sorting out the bill at the cash register. Julia had just waltzed over with the pink ballet bag and begged that it be added to her purchases. I was holding my own plastic bag with the Ballet Emporium logo blazoned in gold letters on the front. I wasn't happy with the canvas shoes and round neck leotard inside it. The pink bag was the last straw. The ballet was my idea in the first place, but I was already falling behind.

I slid the music box with the revolving dancer into my packet to even up the score.

I've never been to a doctor about the habit that I launched that day, but my symptoms seem to fit a description I found online. It describes kleptomania as an impulse disorder. The first symptom is a recurrent failure to resist impulses to steal objects that are not for immediate use or their monetary value. All my stolen goods fit that description perfectly. I didn't look at the price tag on my music box and I never played with it. It was purely a gesture *en route* to equality.

Symptom number two is equally familiar. A kleptomaniac steals without long-term planning and assistance from or collaboration with others. That's also true. It never crossed my mind to take the music box the first time Julia and I watched the dancer spin when we opened up the lid. Julia got bored with it more quickly than I did. She wandered off to look at the rest of the range of toys, but I watched until the music ended. I shut the lid and opened it again. I loved it. I wished it was mine though I never thought of taking it.

Not until Julia got the leather shoes. And the camisole

leotard. And the pink bag with stars and moons.

The third symptom only became familiar as my career progressed. It mentions an increasing sense of tension before committing the act. I became increasingly anxious about getting caught as I grew older, but I didn't feel any tension before I stole the music box. I had no idea that I was going to steal it. My hand just slid out and took it on its own volition. It had some backup from my shifty eyes. They had slithered around to check that no one was looking. I'm sure I could hear my heart beating. It sounded like a drum roll though no one else seemed to hear it. My lungs felt tight and starved of air but somehow my legs started walking when Julia's mom called out that we were done.

"Come on, little ballerinas!" she cried. "Time to go! Mission accomplished!" She tried to take my packet, but I wouldn't let her. "Okay, my darling!" she laughed. "You can carry your own shoes! They're a pretty important purchase, aren't they? Your mom is going to be so excited when she sees what you bought!"

The fourth criterion is always applicable. It says that we kleptos experience either pleasure or release once the theft has been committed. That's what I felt as I settled into the back seat of the car beside Julia, my packet with its forbidden fruit safely clenched between my knees. I would have felt euphoric if I'd known that the word existed. I had a secret. No one in the world knew that I owned a music box with a twirling ballerina. The ballet professor at the Emporium might shake her head and wonder where on earth it went when she came to do a stock-take but no one would remember me.

I expected to be surrounded by the entire police force when I walked out with my loot, but no one sounded the alarm. No one summoned a squad of killer dogs to sniff around and expose my crime.

It was so easy. Anyone would have been encouraged to try again.

> ➤

I was committed to ballet. I was ready and waiting in my leotard and tights every Wednesday afternoon. I sometimes had to fish my kit out of the washing basket, but I never kept Julia's mother waiting. I was like a novitiate at a nunnery, learning to recite a liturgy of prayer in ancient Latin. The holy language in ballet is French.

Glissade. Jete. Entrechat. Fouette. Port de bras.

I heard the words trip off the teacher's tongue. I watched the dancers ease their legs into ever higher extensions. Straight knees and backs. Poised heads and graceful arms. Sliding forwards, backwards and sideways, weight shifting from one foot to the other.

I wished with all my heart that I would turn into one of them, but it was Julia who became the ballet teacher's favorite from the moment she stopped messing around disobediently on the outskirts and took up her position at the barre. It was as if her arms and legs had learned what was expected of them in an earlier life.

I had an entirely different package of genes at my disposal. Not only did I have powerful legs and broad shoulders from my father, but I also had my mother's bottom. I had potential as a hooker on the rugby team or as a San bushman, depending on the angle of the mirror. I was twice as wide as Julia as we looked at our reflections in the studio mirrors. Julia's slim leg could extend upwards almost parallel to her ear. Mine floundered around in the shallows like a beached whale.

One doesn't have to be alive for long to realize that life isn't fair. Ballet taught me that luck levels vary from person to person. It wasn't only the leather shoes and the Doveskin leotard. I could probably have learned to live without a pink ballet bag. The real injustice was that Julia was a better dancer than I was. A deity with any sense of fair play would have doled out talent on someone who was serious about ballet. Someone like me, for instance. Julia clearly didn't value it at all. She would have been just as happy playing rugby in the garden with her multiple brothers and Fatima's multiple sons. Happier in fact, if Karl was on her team. She might have been a Springbok if she'd been fitted out with the right genitals.

I wasn't sufficiently sophisticated to blame my gene pool. I didn't resent my faulty feet. I knew that I had inferior shoes so I stole Julia's. It's easy for a child to steal shoes in South Africa. They blame it on the cleaning staff, even now when apartheid's ended. Julia's leather shoes were sitting beside my canvas pair on the bench as we changed after our lesson finished. I looked at them resentfully when Julia wandered off to the loo. They looked the same as mine but I remembered what Julia's mom had to say about the magical properties of leather. I was sure it spelt the difference between Julia and me.

My shifty eyes darted left and right. I picked up both pairs of shoes and stuffed them into the bottom of the tatty kitbag that I'd inherited from Karl. My stomach tied itself up in knots of guilt when Julia got back from the toilet, but she didn't even notice the shoes were gone.

Her mother though noticed they were missing when she unpacked the bag that evening. My own mother never unpacked my bag so there was no chance she'd register that my ballet shoe collection had doubled in size. I stroked Julia's leather shoes as gently as an Arab stallion. I never danced in them because they were too narrow for me. Cinderella's ugly sisters had much the same problem.

Julia was soon promoted, leaving me to languish with the beginners for a second year. This meant that I had to rely on my mother to collect me after my own lesson finished. It seemed to be against school policy to leave a solitary child in the school carpark so some luckless teacher had to hang around with me until my mother screeched apologetically around the corner. It was even more embarrassing because the secretary sometimes handed me a long white envelope containing a final demand for last month's fees. Everyone heaved a sigh of relief when I announced that I'd decided to give up ballet.

However, I saw no reason to give up stealing at the same time.

➤

SEVEN

My mother had brushed off my suggestions about going to a doctor. Short of bringing in the police, I wasn't quite sure how I was going to get her there but it proved quite simple in the end. She agreed to come along because she needed six stitches in her head. Because she was living on her own, I had no idea that she was starting to struggle to put on her clothes. The blood had already clotted on her head by the time she called me.

"Your phone number got knocked out of my head for a while after the fall!" she laughed as I tried to minister first aid without the help of anything antiseptic like Dettol. She assured me there was Dettol somewhere but it wasn't in any of the places where you might expect to find it and I was afraid the bleeding would start again if I did too much probing. She'd hit her head on the bathroom basin. She'd been trying to put on a pair of jeans.

"And I was feeling so smug that I was losing weight!"

she said. "I'd been hoping that zips wouldn't be such a challenge in future!"

I was really panicking by now. She'd looked much older than her fifty-nine years when I rushed in, after she phoned to tell me about the fall. She'd eventually located her cell and my number is on it which solved the memory lapse complication. She was sitting on the unmade bed, still in her pyjama top with blood on the pillowcase which she'd used to try and stop the bleeding. It was already nearly mid-day but the pyjamas and unmade bed weren't as disturbing as they would have been for someone with a more ordered lifestyle than my mother. It had never been unusual to come home from school and find her watering the pot plants in her pyjamas. Pyjamas to my mother were the equivalent of a tailored jacket to a secretary. They were her work clothes when she was busy with a novel. She always wrote the first draft in longhand, lying on her bed. It wasn't the pyjama top that upset me but she looked thin and neglected.

She looked old.

"Come on Mom," I said tenderly as I helped her slide her legs into the jeans that had caused all the trouble in the first place. Her shoulders seemed frail as I wiped the blood streaks off with warm water and patted them dry with a towel. There were clean towels in the cupboard because I'd phoned Marvellous Maids to come and do a spring clean.

She didn't protest when I phoned the doctor to say that we were on our way. She held onto my arm and let me lead her into his surgery when we arrived. It seemed completely natural for me to sit down beside her after she'd been stitched up and mention that we were worried about her memory lapses.

"There's so much in the papers about Alzheimer's these days..." I trailed off. It seemed like a major hurdle to actually say the word in the presence of a doctor. It put my mother on the defensive immediately.

"*We* aren't worried Dave," she said at once. Dave the doctor had been our family GP for years. He was almost as much a part of the family as Miriam. "I know I probably seem past it to the children but I'm not even sixty yet. And I'm very spry for my age, for that matter. I'm virtually a brainless blonde. I suspect Hannah's making a bid to write me out of the picture so she can get all that money I've got stashed in my offshore account!"

The doctor and I both laughed although it wasn't very funny. Her feistiness made me feel hopeful. I was desperate to hear that I was worrying about nothing but I knew that being fifty -nine didn't put her out of contention for my diagnosis.

My Google search had quoted a couple of extracts from a book by some famous Australian with Alzheimer's who'd written two coherent books since she was diagnosed at forty-eight. Trust the bloody Australians. Their Alzheimer's patients sound as switched on their cricket team. We can never be sure they're beaten, even when the odds are stacked against them. I'd also read that the illness was first diagnosed in some German woman who was fifty-one. The fact that my mother was not yet sixty was more of a worry to me than a consolation. Early-onset Alzheimer's seems even worse because the patients deteriorate more quickly.

I hadn't told Karl how afraid I was that she might die.

The doctor asked us to explain our concerns. Again, my mother denied the existence of any concerns so it was up to me. I felt like Judas when I opened my handbag and handed him a list of the incidents that worried me. I was always urging my mother to make lists of everything she needed to remember. I hadn't told her that I was keeping a list of my own. He read it through in silence. He didn't crumple it into a ball and send us packing.

"I suppose I'll have to bare my veins and let you attack me with a miscellany of needles," said my mother. She was trying hard to keep the tone light and inconsequential.

"I will do some blood tests Chloe," he said gently. "We can get some clarity on other factors that could be causing your symptoms."

My Google search had told me that there's no definitive test for Alzheimer's. Not unless you're dead. A biopsy of the brain will give you any answers you need to know. Dave explained that there were diagnostic tools available, like psychometric tests and scans. I said we'd try everything available. I knew Daniel would make up the deficit with her medical aid.

➤

We became increasingly anxious about Alzheimer's when the blood test results came back. All of them were negative.

"My God," said my mother ruefully. "This is ridiculous. It's as if I'd been praying to have diabetes or sky-high blood pressure. I feel almost disappointed that I'm not HIV-positive. I'd rather have any illness on the planet, other than Alzheimer's," she told me. "Promise you'll push me off a cliff if I get Alzheimer's," she said.

"Don't be so dramatic," I told her. "There are no cliffs in your vicinity. You'll be fine." I refused to contemplate what a positive diagnosis would imply about her future.

"A string of negative blood tests don't prove anything about Alzheimer's," said Karl dismissively when we phoned to tell him the results. He'd also been busy with Google. Even a commune in the Rockies is connected in the new millennium. They probably order the raffia for their mats online. "I still think you're overreacting. You've made your diagnosis and now you're seeing symptoms lurking behind every corner. She sounds exactly the same as ever when I talk to her on the phone."

But she wasn't the same as ever. It's easy to be dismissive when you're living on another continent. The oddness was more related to her behaviour than to her speech at that stage.

I wasn't showing much potential as a geriatric nurse. Iris Murdoch used to drive her husband mad because she kept watering her pot plants. They were close to drowning by the time she'd finished. He'd find her pouring her evening drink onto some luckless waterlogged specimen in the lounge. My mother's problem involved the TV remote and her cell phone. She started getting them mixed up. I would find her sitting on the couch in her inevitable pyjamas, clicking her phone impatiently at the TV.

"Fucking remote," she'd mutter morosely.

"It'll help if you use the remote," I said, handing it to her. I felt like hitting her over the head with it in the end. She would take the remote from me and change the channel but the next time I passed through the lounge, she'd be armed with her cell phone and muttering, "Fucking remote," all over again. It drove me insane.

I thought of a cunning plan to cure her. I phoned her cell from mine. She nearly died of fright when it started to ring in her hand. I could hardly believe it when she put down her ringing phone and answered the remote instead.

"Hello?" she yelled into the remote. "Hello?"

"Fucking cell phone," she muttered as she slammed the remote down on the table beside her and resumed her endless clicking with her phone.

I tried not to lose my temper. I tried to tell myself how frustrating it must be for her. I tried not to be impatient but her cell phone/remote routine drove me up the wall. I didn't realise that I still had a lot to be grateful for. I didn't know how much worse things were going to get. It wasn't very long before she struggled to remember the words for either a cell phone or a remote.

>

EIGHT

I've got a secret drawer where I keep the things I steal.

I knew I had to hide the music box. I didn't have the most conventional of mothers but there were limits. She might not have cared about my school reports or watching X-rated movies, but she would definitely care about stealing. She was such a bad housekeeper that it was easy for me to maintain a secret drawer as a child. I don't think she knew where I kept my underwear.

Everything I've ever stolen is in that drawer. In the order that I stole it. My secret drawer seems deviant even to me, but I can't stop myself. It's the tidiest aspect of my life. The number of items inside it has mounted up though I've never felt the need to deposit them in a Swiss bank vault. They're meaningless to anyone but me. Harmless memorabilia. Even if the lawyer tipped them out and displayed them to the jury, they'd never find me guilty.

No one knows I'm a thief.

I'm very fond of my collection. I know it's a bit offbeat, but no more so than collecting stamps or thimbles. I'm sure a thimble collector likes to browse through her shelf and remember where she bought each piece. That's what I do when I sift through my drawer on rainy days. It's almost like reading a diary.

My music box still works perfectly, after all these years. The music stops abruptly each time I shut the lid and store it away for another rainy afternoon.

>

I was devastated when Julia passed the audition for the Royal Ballet School in London. She was only fifteen. Even Karl and my mother came to the airport the night she left, along with Fatima and all her sons. We didn't lose touch. Julia's parents were devoted to their daughter and mega-rich so they flew her back to Cape Town on a regular basis.

My first attempt at entertaining was less successful than my subsequent career in the field of catering has proved to be. I can now rely on Daniel to whip up a magnificent meal at a moment's notice, but I rashly relied on my mother for Julia's first welcome-home menu.

"It's *flambé*," I explained. "I douse the fillet in brandy and set it alight at the table."

"Dear God," protested Karl. "You better have the fire brigade on standby!"

My mother's reservations were related more to the cost of the fillet and the brandy than to the fire hazard.

She persuaded me to downgrade the meal and adopt an Italian flavor for the evening. "I'll make a divine risotto," she assured me. "And we'll have checked tablecloths and candles and incense."

We had to downgrade the evening even further after my mother burned the rice.

"I told you to put the fire brigade on stand-by," said Karl as my mother scraped the blackened rice into the dust-bin.

"Don't look so tragic, darling," my mother said. "Pizzas are just as Italian as *risotto*. And Italian Kisses for pudding. Even I can't stuff those up."

She bought a bunch of spunky gazanias at the market as penance for the failed risotto and achieved an authentic café atmosphere in the candlelit room. I was easy to placate because I'd never been to Italy. One thing we'd never been short of in Pepper Street was wine glasses and everything looked very sophisticated, once she added the matching serviettes. Julia wouldn't have cared if I'd served up a bowl of sawdust because Karl and his friends were part of the mix. Karl was automatically charming when there were girls around and Julia was sexy, in her Lolita way.

It was well after midnight when Karl and the other guests left, and my mother brought in a tray of cappuccino and the remaining Italian kisses for the three of us. Julia was spending the night so we all changed into our pajamas and snuggled down on the sofas for a chat.

"Was your husband just like Karl?" Julia asked my

mother in a lovelorn tone of voice. She would still have leapt off a cliff for Karl, despite her six-month stint in London.

"Karl looks very much like his father," said my mother. "You can see that from the photos. But they're not really alike, apart from that. Karl was only five when Anton died so he wasn't influenced by him at all when he was growing up. He doesn't even remember him."

"I've always thought it's so romantic that you never married again," sighed Julia. "He was the only one in the world for you..."

My mother just smiled as she ruffled Julia's hair and stroked her cheek. She was very close to Julia. "Oh, my darling," she said. "It's much more romantic to be like your parents. Married to the same person for twenty years."

"But that's so ordinary," protested Julia.

"Ordinary is what I'd choose for Hannah and Karl if a fairy godmother flew in the window and granted me a single wish for their future," my mother replied. But I agreed with Julia.

It would take me another decade to recognize the value of an ordinary life. And an ordinary death.

>

I honed my stealing skills at high school. My stash of stolen goods increased dramatically with the advent of puberty which snuck up on me before I was even officially a teenager. Julia was flat-chested and menstrual-free, as you might expect in a ballet dancer. I was dismayed when it became increasingly obvious that there was yet another category where I had failed to make the grade. I scowled resentfully at my various new extensions as I lounged in the bath each night, although I must concede they broadened my horizons. They opened a new vista of extra mural activities.

I showed more aptitude for sex than I had for ballet. I hooked up with a new best friend after Julia flew off to dance in London. Not a Julia clone. As embryo teens, Julia and I were basically children, but this certainly didn't apply to my new best friend. Karl and his friends called her Mattress Mary. God knows what they called me. Perhaps I was Hannah the Humper. A dash of promiscuity was more a part of our family ethos than ballet. At least my mother didn't have to budget for the fees.

Mattress Mary evolved in an environment which couldn't have been more different from Julia's home-cooked meals and maternal devotion. Mary's mom was a highflier. A successful entrepreneur with a finger in the international pie. Frequently away from home. Their au-pair was as lax about curfews as my mother, so Mary and I had plenty of time to prowl, to add more notches than anyone would expect to find on the average teenage belt.

Mattress Mary came over as a higher profile tart than me – perhaps because she was spawned by a higher profile mother who looked consistently expensive in her tailored suits and her Audi. Back at home in Pepper Street, hunched over her ageing laptop, my mother looked more like a mobile jumble sale. One might conclude that dress sense is as genetic as Alzheimer's, if Mary and I were included in the sample study.

Mary makes an impression, but not because she's beautiful. Somehow, she warrants a second glance with her horn-rimmed glasses, her flawless olive skin, luxurious dark hair pulled back from her face into a careless bun – until the DJ turns up the volume and she lets it down...

Maybe that's the link between her and Julia. They're both dancers – but Julia is into ballet. Her movements seem impossibly graceful. Fluid, but always disciplined. She practises every single day. You know exactly what to expect from Julia when the curtain goes up. Mary is different. Just as fluid but her essence is sensual. You'd think it would clash with the horn-rimmed glasses, but somehow they seem to add a dimension. Like the hair that escapes from the bun on her neck. Watching Mary dance suggests that she's worth pursuing.

I warranted a line of suitors of my own. I had more seduction potential than I initially realized. Beauty is overrated by poets and novelists. They wax lyrical about flawless faces, but all you really need to launch a thousand ships is big tits. I have to thank my mother for my primary assets. She may not have delivered the genes I needed to launch a career in ballet, but she was well equipped in the breast vicinity. A hug from her felt like sinking into a goose-down duvet. Hugging Julia's mother was a different experience entirely, with all her lines and angles.

I became pretty huggable myself once I hit puberty.

Big tits are a primary target when the suitors in question are teenage boys. They don't really care about interesting conversation which was a fringe benefit if you made progress with Mary. The one who valued this aspect of Mary's persona was my mother. I sometimes sulked in my bedroom, brooding that the main reason Mary dropped into Pepper Street might be to chat to my mother. About the books they were reading. About politics. Whatever.

Mary loved my mother – and Julia loved my brother. I sometimes wondered where I ranked in the pecking order with my best friends.

That was a big plus factor with Daniel. I was the only one who could deliver a multiple orgasm.

➤

I was surprised by my family's opposition to my new direction, in the light of their general enthusiasm for sex. A dash of promiscuity was a birthright they seemed determined to deny me. The age of consent seemed to be about forty in my case. It wasn't fair. My mother often rounded off an evening of wine-fueled laughs and conversation by leading her current professor off to bed. Karl and I didn't blink an eyelid when we found another genial old fellow, eating cornflakes beside us at the breakfast table.

Karl wasn't an abstemious role model either. He was captain of the rugby team and the Camel Man factor was an advantage. There was always a procession of girls draped over him in our lounge. It seemed entirely unreasonable for both Karl and my mother to turn into paragons of chastity at the prospect of anyone seducing me.

I've got the classic Stanley Kubrick movie of *Lolita* in my DVD collection. It's pretty dated now. I like black and white movies though. It has an understated opening with Humbert's hand holding Lolita's small delicate foot. He's painting her toenails. You see his fingers separating each toe. His old hand on her young foot. It's a decadent story. I added the DVD to my collection because it reminded me of the night I became aware of the power of my newly developed assets.

My mother's lovers were mostly old academics. I'm making them sound more shrivelled than they really were. And it's not as if there was a new one every night. Ian was around for several years and so was Andrew. Both of them were quite attractive – like Humbert in a way but not as seedy. They were certainly several decades older than me. I was no older than Lolita. Our age was the only thing we had in common. A boyish outline wasn't part of my portfolio.

I'd caught the eye of a new man in my mother's life. Llewellyn Stone. I'll always remember it. He was one of those men who age well. I can still remember his lean face. He had blue eyes and long fingers. His hands were beautiful. Mary had just introduced me to shaving my legs. I can remember feeling relieved that my legs were smooth and hairless when I felt his fingers stroke them. I wasn't remotely like Lolita. Her seaside limbs. Apple-sweet. There was nothing slim and graceful about my legs, even though I'd just moved into the teenage era. Julia was more like Lolita with her lean androgynous body and her unconscious grace. There was something sensual about Julia, even when she was a little girl. I should have noticed the way Karl and his friends looked at her.

I noticed Llewellyn looking at me as I breezed through the lounge in my Woolies nightshirt to watch an episode of *Falcon Crest*. I loved *Falcon Crest*. My mother dismissed it scornfully though she watched it as avidly as I did. My Woolies nightie was T-shirt material and I'd only given myself a cursory dry when I got out of the shower. I didn't want to miss a moment of my favorite soap. My mother didn't notice how the nightie clung to my damp body, warm from the shower. I was her baby. In her slapdash way, she hadn't really noticed that I could have a baby myself, if I took the pre-requisite steps.

No baby of mine would have gone hungry. I could have fed an entire platoon from the army, even in my early teens. My mother may not have noticed anything bouncing around under my nightie but Llewellyn certainly did. I couldn't give *Falcon Crest* the attention it deserved once I became aware that he was watching me. I could hardly wait to tell Mary.

"He couldn't take his eyes off me!" I bragged which wasn't strictly true. Off them I should have said. It certainly wasn't my face with its very aquiline nose that had caught his eye. It was my eager nipples and my newly shaven thighs. I'd thought of them both as impediments up till then. Both my breasts and thighs were far too big for my liking, but Llewellyn obviously preferred large to lean. There was nothing lean about my mother and she was his primary target. I was merely a side-show for Llewellyn. I'm sure he wasn't a pervert, but I'd never heard of Lolita. I was simply flattered that a man was looking at me with unmistakable interest.

"Sit next to him on the couch next time he comes round," suggested Mary. "See what happens."

"But he's so old!" I protested. "He's as old as my mother!"

"It might be interesting," said Mary enigmatically. "More experience you know..." Mary claimed to have learned a lot from some uncle or stepfather. I can't remember the details but she made it sound exciting rather than sordid.

I thought it was worth following up on Llewellyn. Opportunity knocked one evening when my mother popped down to the café to get some groceries she'd overlooked. She had a long history of overlooking groceries. I was often left with either Karl or a visiting friend or suitor while she made her lightning dash. I knew I'd have to get stuck into my Llewellyn project pretty quickly if I was hoping to seduce him before she got back with the bread and milk.

I settled down beside him on the sofa, my toxic assets bobbing freely under my nightie. I tucked my legs up underneath me so my nightie rose up to expose the rest of my armory. Well, it exposed my thighs. I hadn't yet given any real thought to the role of my vagina in a seduction package. I heard Llewellyn swallow. Ah ha, I thought, he's weakening. I felt irresistible as I slid my foot onto his lap and arranged my lips in an amateur version of a pout. I didn't feel quite so in control of the situation when Llewellyn rested his hand on my foot. That's how Lolita starts. That's why it struck a chord the first time I watched it. I started to panic when he slowly moved his fingers up my freshly shaven leg. His beautiful lean fingers. Immaculate fingernails...

I'll never know how far up he would have moved them because Karl arrived home at that inauspicious moment. Both Llewellyn and I nearly jumped out of our respective skins as he came barging into the lounge. I knew I was going to be saddled with my virginity for a while longer when I saw Karl register the scene on the couch. My legs across Llewellyn's lap. His hand under my nightie.

I knew his outrage was nothing compared to the way my mother would react when she got home with the loaves and fishes. I'd be lucky to get away with the death penalty. I was filled with dread once I'd flounced petulantly off to my room when Karl sent Llewellyn on his way in no uncertain terms.

My heart flinched when my mother opened my bedroom door. I was expecting her to be armed with the garden axe, but her reaction was entirely different from Lolita's mother's. She didn't say a word. I thought she must be speechless with rage until I felt myself pressed against her own sizable bosom. Her hand stroked my hair gently.

"I'm so sorry, darling girl," she whispered.

My ears nearly fell off in surprise. It didn't sound like

the death sentence was imminent after all. She was indeed speechless with rage, but it wasn't directed at me. Llewellyn is the one who should have been shaking in his shoes. He's lucky she didn't have him arrested and thrown into Pollsmoor.

I didn't value her reaction at the time. I just mopped my brow and rolled my eyes as I told Mary how I'd gotten away unscathed. I was too young to appreciate that I was lucky. All I knew was that I was still a virgin. I wished that Llewellyn had kissed me, at the very least.

➤

It was the virginity issue that forced me to resort to shoplifting again. I thought it would be easier to lose if I was wearing a G-string rather than one of the six-pack of large beige panties from Woolworths which is what my mother always came home with when I told her I needed new underwear. My bras also came in budget packs. They too were beige and designed more in terms of support than a display of cleavage. If I ever did find someone who wanted to undress me, he'd be completely turned off when he reached my underwear. I'd be a virgin forever with my unsatisfactory body togged out in beige undies.

Mary's underwear drawer was very different from mine. It boasted a miscellany of skimpy bras and panties in all the colors of the bloody rainbow. You could see the top of her G-string above her low-slung jeans. They sell plenty of G-strings, even at Woolworths. My mother could have bought them just as easily as a beige six-pack, I thought morosely.

I stole a G-string from a Waterfront boutique. What option did I have? I needed a G-string. It was like a badge of honor in the police force. As with the music box, I acted purely on impulse. The music box heist had happened so long ago that I'd forgotten about shoplifting as a route to get something that you don't have and can't afford. The G-string incident was the first time that I tried the diversion tactics that were to serve me so well.

I had some time to kill. I strolled into the boutique because I'd been afflicted with an underwear fetish. The boutique sold imported lingerie. The Waterfront's target market is foreign tourists so they don't blink an eyelid at prices that make Woolworths look like a bargain basement. There were racks of tasteful morsels of lace and silk. They looked like certain winners for anyone bent on seduction. I lingered over a scarlet G-string with a tiny triangle of scarlet lace in front. It would knock the socks off any male on the planet.

I looked at the tag. Over two hundred rand! It was imported from Italy. It might as well have cost a hundred million as far as my budget was concerned. It was triple the price of an entire beige six-pack. My eyes slotted into shifty mode. The solitary saleslady was looking through another rack for a customer trying on a range of bras behind the curtain.

Without a second thought – or even a first for that matter – I knocked over the whole stand of Italian imports. It made an impressive clunk as it dumped its fragile load of lace and silk on the floor. The sales lady looked as if war had just been declared. I suppose there's not much market for underwear that's been lying on the floor. She was beside me in seconds as I scrabbled to pick up the garments.

"Leave it to me!" she yelled, as if my fingernails were dirty.

She wasn't looking at me when she struggled to restore the stand to an upright position. I cunningly hooked a finger around my target G-string. It was tiny so it slipped into my handbag in a heartbeat. I was terrified that my errant finger had been recorded on a camera. My heart was pounding when I disappeared onto the crowded walkway.

>

I didn't brag about my shoplifting skills. They have always been my secret. They haven't been an unqualified success, despite the fact that I've managed to avoid a criminal record. I've never worn Julia's ballet shoes because they were too small and my scarlet G-string panties fared no better.

I'd look better in a raincoat than a G-string, I decided glumly as I slipped on my spoils behind my locked bedroom door. I'd have to steal a bikini-wax kit as well if I was hoping to tempt a lover in my scarlet Italian panties. I didn't look as sexy as I hoped with a tangle of unpruned curls bristling out on all sides of the triangle at the front and my large bottom looming at the rear.

I should have stolen a scarlet bra as well if I was to have any hope of success. My scarlet triangle looked ridiculous teamed up with a beige bra from Woolies. I tore it off and wrenched open my secret drawer. I stuffed the scarlet wisp of silk angrily into the toe of one of the ballet shoes. I never wanted to see it again. It reinforced everything I didn't like about my teenage body.

I accumulated nearly a dozen other items of clothing in my secret drawer before I abandoned my shoplifting hobby. I never wore any of them because they were all far too small. Sexy bras and panties. A couple of bikinis. A slinky red dress, made to mold itself onto your body like a second skin. I stole that just before the Matric dance that I had to go to with a partner that I didn't like, wearing a dress I hated. It felt as if all my dreams were going to stay in my secret drawer forever.

NINE

I went with my mother to the Constantiaberg Clinic the day we booked an MRI with a local radiologist. Dr. Dave had assured us that their machines were as up-to-date as anywhere in the world. The healthcare sector in South Africa has had international standing since the days when Christian Barnard started swopping hearts between patients at Groote Schuur.

We were both nervous. I'd never had an MRI myself but the ever-reliable Google delivered the information complete with photos. It looked rather like a concentration camp device to me, with some poor patient lying prostrate on a metal table before disappearing inside a tunnel. I'm not sure whether the CT scan sounded better or worse. They inject you with some low-grade radioactive substance which highlights what's going on inside your head. It sounds insane but I was almost hoping they would find a tumor. Just a little tumor. At least you can cut out a tumor.

My stomach clenched when Dr. Dave's receptionist phoned to make an appointment. My mother and I were both artificially cheerful on our way to keep it, but we knew the news couldn't be good. Dr. Dave would have phoned himself if it had been.

"Nothing to worry about here, Chloe!" he would have boomed in his cheery way. But he didn't do that, so we both knew we had plenty to worry about.

X-rays always come in big brown envelopes. I didn't reach over to hold my mother's hand when Dr. Dave opened it and laid the X-rays on the table in front of us. I thought that holding her hand would confirm that I was feeling frightened. I'm scared of X-rays. They're so invasive, with their sinister ability to penetrate beneath the surface and lay the truth bare for everyone to see. It's like breaking a trust. Telling a secret. I didn't really want to hear about the secrets my mother's body was holding.

Dave's face was serious as he talked. Our family had been going to see him for years with flu and sprained ankles and upset tummies. I know he liked all three of us, but he was particularly fond of my mother. She was that sort of person. She was entertaining company, even through a stethoscope.

"I'm not going to pretend that there's no cause for concern," he said. "This scan looks as if it's the brain of someone older than you are, Chloe," he continued. He pointed out an area in one of the shades of grey. "There are signs of atrophy in this frontal area. The brain size is smaller than it should be." He pointed out two dark areas. They looked like two black holes lurking somewhere in the spaces of the universe. They looked empty. "These are the ventricles," he said. "Larger than normal."

There was a silence before my mother asked the question I was trying to evade because I'd already read the answer on my Google search.

"This atrophy. The enlarged ventricles. Are they something you'd expect to find with Alzheimer's?"

He didn't avoid the question. I suppose its part and parcel of the Hippocratic Oath not to lie to your patients about a terminal disease. He said he wanted to set up an appointment with a psychiatrist to carry out psychometric tests specifically designed to test memory. I did take her hand when he mentioned the memory tests because we both knew she'd fail.

➤

"I think those tests were designed by someone with a personal vendetta against me," complained my mother when I collected her after she'd spent the afternoon closeted with the psychiatrist. "They focused on all my specific weaknesses. I had to memorize grocery lists, for Christ's sake. Grocery lists are a closed book to me. I've always treated supermarkets like a nuclear hazard. I never come home with everything we need from Pick n Pay!"

My mother sounded so reassuringly familiar that I was lulled into a sense of false security. She admitted that she was completely baffled by the electronic maze they'd asked her to try and negotiate her way around.

But direction had never been one of her strengths. She couldn't find her way home from the airport after all. Maybe Alzheimer's wouldn't be so bad, even if she did have it. My mother was as mad as a hatter, at the best of times. Maybe we wouldn't even notice.

>-

Dr. Dave organized a genetic screening blood test when he read the psychiatrist's report, which suggested that my mother showed signs of MCI: Mild Cognitive Impairment. A whole range of acronyms had suddenly taken on new meaning for me.

"Does having this MCI thing mean she's definitely going to get Alzheimer's?" asked Karl when I made my regular phone call to tell him about the latest test results.

Our situation improved as time passed and Skype became ubiquitous. The biggest plus with Skype is not that it's free. It's the visuals. It felt like Karl was in the room next door when I talked to him. And even more important, he could see that there was something different about our mother, even when her conversation sounded normal. Her body language showed that she'd started to withdraw into herself, even in those early stages. Talking to my mother on Skype helped Karl to come to terms with the fact that she was really sick.

"Not everyone with MCI gets Alzheimer's," I told him, "but she will almost definitely get it. Dave sent in another blood test for a genetic screening and she's got a double copy of APO-E."

"Dear God," said Karl. "You keep throwing all these bloody terms into the conversation. Do you have any idea what they all mean? What the hell's APO?"

"I can't actually remember," I admitted. "Dave explained it all but it sounds like Latin. I have no idea what it stands for. I think it's a blood type when you get down to basics. It's a gene that you inherit. You can get a copy from either parent. Or a copy from each. Mom's got a double copy, and that's the problem. If you have even one copy, you're three or four times more times at risk for Alzheimer. If you've got a double copy, it would be extremely unlikely for you not to get Alzheimer's."

"My God," said Karl again. "The future doesn't sound too rosy for us either, does it?"

"Well, we can't do much about it," I answered. "Dave says your APO status is coded into your genetic make-up at the moment of conception. We can't get it flushed out. It's lurking there like a nuclear bomb. At present anyway. They've still got thirty years to find a cure before we get to that stage."

"Only twenty-five years for me," corrected Karl.

I didn't yet have the courage to tell him that it was already too late for our mother. Dave had told us that a double copy of APO-E predicted a very aggressive form of Alzheimer's. Even with the best medication currently available on the international market, she could go downhill very rapidly. She could die within three years. Sooner, if she had her way. My mother kept insisting that the time for pushing her off a cliff was imminent.

She forgot about the cliff option when her symptoms intensified.

TEN

It's just as well my mother boycotted school functions. The head might have had her burned for heresy if he'd overheard the career guidance she spewed out to the children in her life. She claimed that it was a mistake to become irrevocably committed to a career before you knew what you really wanted to do with your life. She was horrified when Mattress Mary told us that she'd signed up for actuarial science at UCT. Mary must have paid attention when her mother dished out advice about earning a fortune in the high-powered world she moved in every day. My own mother behaved as if the luckless girl had opted for sadomasochism or vivisection.

"Your soul will shrink if you become an actuary!" she warned her darkly. "And you'll feel obliged to be an actuary all your life because it will take you about a decade to qualify! Think very carefully before you commit yourself, my darling!"

This was quite an original line of thought for a parent but it suited me. I liked the prospect of avoiding exams entirely in my future. University lectures held no appeal because I've never been a morning person. Our friends delivered pizza while they studied to get the qualifications needed to follow in their father's footsteps. But we didn't have a father and our mother only left intermittent footprints because of her limp. Pizzas were a full-time career for Karl until he became a global traveler. I became a waitress. I like to think of it as my foundation stage.

I kept different hours from my friends. I was sound asleep in the mornings when Mary was sitting on the Jammie steps at UCT after an early morning lecture. We didn't lose touch because she was a waitress too, but she only worked once or twice a week to boost her cash flow. I was far richer than her at that stage. Her earning potential became a lot healthier than mine once she qualified, but you can earn a fortune in a restaurant in the right location.

I had no reservations about the way I made a living. I earned enough to buy a student ticket to fly to Croatia with my mother. We were both desperate to catch up with the global traveler in our family. He'd been working his way around the continent for years by then. Julia had seen more of him in London than we had in Cape Town.

She and I had remained as close as the sisters that neither of us had, despite the ocean in between us. Brothers are taboo for real sisters, but Julia never shelved her pre-adolescent crush on Karl. I had no room to criticize. I'd taken her trio of brothers for granted until the second eldest joined the queue of adolescent boys eager to take advantage of my reputation. It had started to burgeon after I eventually disposed of my virginity in the backseat of one of Julia's family fleet of cars.

"You slept with Peter?" howled Julia in disbelief. I had sneaked into the lounge to make a long-distance confession after my mother had gone to bed.

"He was drunk!" I whispered, drenched with shame. Peter was hardly a conquest, with his skinny legs and problem skin. I'd been pretty drunk myself but I was reluctant to accept any responsibility for what seemed more like incest than a sensual adventure.

"You have to be more discriminating," said Julia sternly. I noticed that she shelved her reservations about semi-sibling sex pretty quickly when Karl called her up in London because he needed a room for the night.

"It's not the same as you and Peter!" she protested when I pointed out her inconsistencies. "I love Karl! You know I've always loved Karl!"

"Make an effort not to," I warned her. I knew my brother. Karl specialized in breaking hearts and moving on. Moving on was a way of life for Karl.

"Leave Julia alone!" I yelled in fury when he called from London to see how his mother and sister were coping without a man around the house. "You can't mess her around like all the others!"

He just laughed before he put the phone down. "Little Jules is all grown up!" he assured me. "Living in London does that to a girl. She's learned a lot since you last saw her!"

She hadn't learned as much as he thought. She didn't sound at all grown up in the series of tearful phone calls I got from her after Karl moved out of her flat. He kissed her goodbye as soon as he decided it was time to explore a different continent. A succession of different continents. A succession of different versions of Julia who finally conceded that she'd had a lucky escape. She found a new boyfriend and the tearful midnight phone calls petered out. She only phoned after midnight if something was bothering her.

The most significant of her midnight calls was more recent. I'd returned from London with my tail between my legs because my visa had expired. At the time, I didn't register that it was a call that needed my attention. It was prior to the advent of my Iris-eyes.

She phoned me to talk about her lunch date with my mother. Mom had gone to England to visit her English relations who were getting older and dying off like flies. I should have listened more carefully to what Julia had to say, but I wasn't at my most receptive when I picked up the phone. It may have been mid-summer in London, but Cape Town was in the throes of a series of cold fronts with their typical rain and freezing temperatures. I couldn't find my slippers and my feet were frozen solid.

"Why are you phoning in the middle of the night?" I snarled.

"Don't be so unfriendly," she replied. "My motives are

good. I met your mom for lunch. I'm worried about her."

"What's happened?" I asked, suddenly more awake. My mother was prone to getting into trouble, long before she had Alzheimer's.

"No, no," she said. "Don't panic. She's fine. I'm sure she's fine. But it was odd. It's been bothering me. I wondered if it's something you've noticed too. I must have told her I'm in the chorus in Giselle about four times during lunch. Then she'd tell me how much you loved your first matinee with my mom and me."

"And so?" I said, "what's wrong with that? Is that what I've been woken up to hear?"

"Well, it was fine the first time," said Julia. "But ten minutes later, she asked me again. And again. And she trotted out the whole matinee anecdote every time. Almost word for word. It was really disconcerting."

"Oh please." I said dismissively. "I can't believe you've got me out of bed in a blizzard to tell me that my mother's mad. You know my mother's mad. She's been consistently mad for as long as you've known her. Even longer. She's always been mad."

"Not like this," said Julia. "She's more eccentric than mad. But this was really strange. It was different. Out of character."

But I dismissed it. It seemed like a non-event to me. Not enough to keep me away from my warm bed in the middle of the night in winter Cape Town. I feel guilty about that phone call now. I shelved that conversation along with a miscellany of other hints that only became significant in retrospect.

Perhaps it doesn't matter. I couldn't have changed the future, even if I'd paid more attention to the present and the past.

ELEVEN

I harboured a dark secret which I never admitted to my mother, especially when I found that it was shared by my brother. We were so ashamed of the truth that we didn't even want to admit it to each other. I thought I was the only guilty one. I would never have admitted it to anyone, not even if the police had tried to pry it out of me with a crowbar in one of their notorious holding cells.

I've never read the *Not-So-Famous-Five*.

I brag about them all the time whenever a new acquaintance finds out that I'm Chloe Cartwright's daughter. I know the titles and the basic stories, but I've never actually been able to plow all the way through one. I've never been an avid reader. Karl and I lounged our youth away on a couch in front of the television. We kept such midnight hours that we were too tired to read a book before we went to bed. I read magazines and go to movies. I never read novels about the political throes of South Africa.

I've read enough of Karl's school reports to know that his reading skills were as minimal as mine, but we were already adults when I asked him whether he'd read the Not-So-Famous-Five. I asked him in Croatia, of all places. Maybe I wanted to be certain no one we knew could overhear our conversation. Maybe it was because everyone in Croatia seems to be Catholic. Perhaps confession is contagious.

We went to Croatia in the first spring of the new millennium. It had taken me two years to save the fare. It's hard to save if your only income is the tips the customers don't always deliver. I had to buy the ticket on my card and pay it off in small bites. Karl had some menial job in Zagreb. My mother was particularly motivated to join him because Croatia was still behind the Iron Curtain when she and my father explored Europe in the sixties with flowers in their hair. As an activist and a journalist, my mother was eager to make some contact with other people who'd also taken the momentous step to end oppression. Perhaps she thought she'd cover the airfare with some freelance articles when she got back.

Croatia will always be an indelible memory for me because it was the first overseas holiday the three of us had together as a family. It was virtually the first holiday we'd had together anywhere. Ballet lessons weren't the only thing my mother couldn't afford while we were growing up. It was wonderful to be together in a foreign city!

We wandered past ancient buildings and soaring

*church spires in the religious heart of Zagreb. We no-
ticed chattering groups of blue- and black-clad nuns
as we soaked in the silence of the cathedral with its
vaulted gothic arches and stained-glass windows.
People knelt in silent prayer as they lit their candles
of hope and remembrance. It looked as if they were
all busy confessing, left, right and center. No wonder I
spilled the beans to Karl.*

I remember the night as clearly as if I'd made my confession to the Pope himself. We met a group of South African academics in the bar. They'd read my mother's novels, and they pounced on her as if they'd unearthed a rare archaeological treasure. Karl and I were left sipping our East European beers at a table in a pavement café. We could hear my mother and her new academic soulmates waxing on about her novels at the adjoining table.

"Have you ever read her books?" I asked him baldly. He looked outraged.

"How can you ask me that, for Christ's sake? We've been surrounded by books under construction all our lives!"

"Well, I haven't read them," I confessed on impulse. I lowered my voice, as if I was admitting to a heinous crime. "I've tried but I always feel like I'm drowning by about page three. I don't have the stamina to persevere."

"Really?" said Karl, sounding incredulous. "You always sound as if you've read them."

"Well, so do you," I said. "I've just read the covers. And

I read the reviews. That's all you need to get you through a conversation. It's like a study guide on Macbeth. No one expects you to say anything profound."

Karl looked amazed. "That's exactly what I do!" he said. "Maybe everyone does that. Maybe no-one's ever read them except the panel who hands out the prizes!"

I'm sure that's not true. There are plenty of people with more depth to their reading habits than my mother's shallow children. She was a serious writer, even though she's as mad as a hatter when she's not in front of a computer. She won the Alan Paton award for non-fiction and a Pen award for one of her short stories. She's also been shortlisted for some other big deal fiction prize a couple of times, though she didn't win it on either occasion. Her books revolve around her years as a political activist, both before apartheid ended and during the transition.

I can't face a book about apartheid and the struggle. Her books are all about five hundred pages long. The covers show haunted faces of disadvantaged children or star-crossed lovers of illegal colors. I prefer Bridget Jones or a good thriller laced with sex and murder and the odd mutilation. But I'd die rather than admit it to anyone other than Karl. My mother wasn't a model mother, but we weren't model children either. We didn't have much time left when we recognized our shortcomings.

❧

I may not have read any of my mother's novels, but I developed my own singular line of support. I stole her books.

I wanted her to think that someone was buying them.

She had her own version of an obsessive-compulsive disorder while we were growing up in Pepper Street. She used to count the copies of her books whenever she dropped into a bookshop.

Books are harder to steal than panties because they don't slide into a handbag as easily. I'm rather proud of the fact that my serial book thefts didn't earn me a criminal record. I like to believe it's because I was too crafty to get caught. I'd hate to think that no one cared that my mother's books were missing from their shelves. She was always so optimistic when the royalty checks arrived from Penguin.

"Ah ha!" she'd yell when she saw the familiar emblem and ripped the envelope in her haste to see what it contained. "I think we're into the money now, kiddos!" she'd enthuse, her body language emitting hope like a hundred-watt globe. She was always wrong. Her books remained in print because she'd won so many prizes. There's always some literary aficionado or politician who wants a copy now and then, but it's hard for a local author to make any money if she writes politically correct social commentaries. An ivory-tower academic might value her lyrical prose, but most people are like Karl and me. They prefer Bridget Jones and Steig Larsson.

I remember stealing the first of my mother's books because it's the only theft that made me feel guilty. That was because of the venue. Clarke's Bookshop on Long Street is an institution in Cape Town. It's just a short walk from our house in Pepper Street. I've known the owner for years.

"Are you looking for anything in particular, Hannah?" she asked me as I climbed up the stairs while she and my mom settled down for tea and a chat in the office.

"Just browsing!" I said cheerily. I didn't know I was about to steal. I made my way to the shelf my mother always visited the moment we arrived at Clarke's. The book was still there, Chloe Cartwright blazoned on the cover. I remember how she'd sighed when she saw it the last time we came.

"It's still here," she said glumly as she put it back in place. "It'll be here forever. No one's ever going to buy it." I took it down from the shelf. I felt sad that my mother's book had attracted so little interest. It was in perfect condition. It didn't look as if anyone had paged through it or lingered over a particular section. No thumbprints or stains that you might find in a book that's been savored and reread. I slid off my school rucksack, my shifty eyes slithering to the left and right. I could hear my mother and Lydia laughing in the office. And hey, presto, within seconds the book was alongside my homework in the rucksack! I felt wracked with guilt when I stood beside Lydia to say goodbye. She smiled as she gave me my customary kiss and hug on my way out. Some people don't make stealing easy.

>

I'd left school by the time I plucked up enough courage to steal from one of the chain stores. I targeted Longfellow Books at the Gardens Center because my mother was a regular customer. She always dropped in on her way to

Woolworths or Pick n Pay to see if any copies had been sold. She was particularly downcast the night I made my first strike. That's why I did it. We were at some random book launch. She sighed as if the world had ended when she saw her own books squatting on the shelf, a grim reminder of her lack of sales. I felt sorry for her.

Everyone was jostling for access to free wine and snacks. The public always reverts to hunter-gatherer mode if there's anything in limited supply that's going free. They were wolfing down slivers of pizza and cocktail sausages and snapping up books for signing. No one would have noticed if I'd taken off all my clothes and launched into a can-can. I slipped the book into the ever-ready rucksack and joined the throng at the snacks. She phoned me when she came back with her groceries the next week.

"Someone's bought one!" she crowed. "I think the tide is turning!"

I added another one to my drawer after my next outing to Exclusive Books in Cavendish. Their security is pretty suspect because they've got the Seattle coffee shop keyed into the equation. Some of the tables are outside the shop. People pick up books and magazines and page through them over a cup of coffee. The carrot cake's not bad either.

I wasn't planning to steal the copy of one of my mother's books in the section on South African literature. I was merely going to move it to a more prominent position, after I placed my regulation order for coffee and cake. I did note, however, that there was no one in sight. I drained my cup and picked up a few stray crumbs which had escaped my attention. No one made any attempt to stop me as I sauntered off down the corridor with my mother's book clearly on display for anyone to see.

Those three copies of my mother's books are stored beside the underwear in my secret drawer. I stopped stealing them after that because it seemed a pointless exercise. I'd have to steal a whole truck load of books to make any difference in her royalties. I might have persevered if she'd written some thinner versions, but it's challenge to slink out of a shop with one of my mother's weighty tomes.

I knew I'd wasted my time the day she unlocked my secret drawer. She didn't ask why the books were there.

She didn't remember writing them.

➤

There's a strange finality about the fact that the only two European capitals we visited as a family both begin with Z. The cities certainly don't have much else in common. Zurich airport didn't remind me of Zagreb's. Everything works like clockwork at Zurich.

Despite the slick efficiency of the Swiss, I remember much more about Zagreb than I do about Zurich. We had to hire a car in Zurich, which was just another city. I have barely any memory of it, but I can still visualise a number of random details about Zagreb.

One memory in particular stands out: a pocket of silence that we came across in a narrow alley. Kamenita

Vrata. A gate set in stone, housing a sixteenth-century painting of the Holy Virgin, which had miraculously survived fire and is reputed to have the power to heal. A tanned young man in shorts and a T-shirt was kneeling in front of it, his head bowed. He looked incongruous in the setting. He would have seemed more at home on a yacht in the Caribbean. I wonder if his prayer was answered?

If I'd had any insight into the future, I would have gotten down onto my knees and prayed with him. Perhaps the Virgin could have helped us too?

I'd have asked her to take Zurich out of our future itinerary.

TWELVE

I'd never take London out of my itinerary. I was eager to extend my European experience after we returned from our Croatian jaunt in 2000. Mattress Mary had completed her first degree en route to her actuarial goal. There's a high dropout rate in that branch of business science because you have to get an insanely high mark to pass. She had to work for another few years to qualify as a fully fledged actuary, but fortunately Mary had stamina to match her brain power. She thought her qualification would be improved if her work experience was in London so we applied for two-year work permits to join Julia in her Kensington flat in London. She was dancing full-time with some high-profile ballet company by then.

Mary and I had only been in London a week before we bought tickets to watch Julia dance in *Swan Lake* at the Royal Albert Hall. It seemed inconceivable that we were at such an illustrious venue as we took our seats and looked up at the domed ceiling above us.

"A friend of ours is dancing tonight," I confided to the luckless stranger who was trying to read her program in the seat beside me.

"Be quiet!" hissed Mary as the orchestra struck up the familiar score. The curtains parted on the set that had become familiar over the years. It seemed as if a century had passed since Julia and I started ballet lessons in the studio in suburban Cape Town.

"There she is!" I whispered to the luckless stranger, clutching her arm as the swans glided onto the stage and took up their impossibly graceful positions. Julia had shrugged off her achievement as one of the lower profile swans in the production. We knew better. Only the most talented of swans make it onto the stage at the Royal Albert Hall. We were riveted by her contribution. She was the standout swan in our eyes. We hoped any talent scouts in the audience that night were as perceptive. We rose in our seats to applaud when the final curtain fell!

"Congratulate your friend from me," gushed my luckless stranger as she made her way out of the theater. She seemed to have grown quite fond of both Julia and me during the course of the production.

The staff at the employment agency also grew quite fond of me by the time I eventually found a job. They didn't have time to get fond of Mary because she was snapped up immediately by some impressive investment bank to do God-knows-what on their behalf. She took her job seriously. I'd never imagined Julia dancing for the National Ballet, but even that was less unlikely than Mattress Mary's evolution. I used to moan and groan because she woke me up every morning. She always turned the radio on to listen to the stock exchange report on the BBC while she got dressed for her job in the city.

"How can you have turned into a banker?" I howled, with the pillow over my head to shut out both the light and the radio. "I far preferred you when you were a bonker."

"Bankers still bonk," she assured me as she clunked around in our mutual cupboard to find a suitably tailored outfit to match her laptop and leather briefcase. "I move into bonking mode after office hours. You can watch me in action at the Coachman tonight!" she called as she slammed the front door and set off into the London drizzle to join the queue at the tube station.

I pulled the duvet more warmly around me and tried to get back to sleep. Thank God I wasn't on a morning shift. I'd finally landed a job at the Coachman where my waitressing non-career continued to thrive until my visa expired. The passport office rejected my application to renew it.

"The bastards!" wailed Julia as she read through my letter with its bureaucratic stamp. She and Mary had both had their visas renewed as highly skilled immigrants or whatever the classification was for people who could make a contribution to the British economy. Julia had already been in London for long enough to get British citizenship. No doubt Mary would soon follow in her footsteps. I would be the only one without a British passport which allows its lucky owners to go anywhere without the complication of a visa. I was glum about the festive weekends I'd miss when Julia and Mary went swanning off to Paris and Amsterdam on a moment's notice. It was some years before I'd need to visit Zurich on short notice.

I was philosophical when Julia and Mary waved me goodbye at Heathrow. I settled into my window seat to brood about the future. In some ways, I was glad to be going home. I was sick of the rain and the gloomy Brits and the endless journeys underground on crowded tubes. Not to mention the lack of knights in shining armor. I'd look for one on Clifton beach.

I'd loved London with its mix of ancient history and new millennium traffic, but it's not Cape Town. I can't believe that England will ever seem like home to Julia or Mary or anyone who grew up in the shadow of our famous mountain. Karl says he'll always be African, however seldom he comes here now.

But I must admit to an unfamiliar stab of anxiety as I looked out the window on the long flight home and thought about my past. The visa issue upset me. Julia and Mary had no trouble getting theirs. I had to admit they'd worked hard to acquire their status. Julia's life as a dancer was pure slog. Long hours of practice. Rehearsals. Competition. Late nights. And look at Mary. You deserve more than a visa if you're an actuary. God knows what an actuary does. It sounds like a truly dreadful way to spend the day. I just had to jot down a few orders and flirt with the customers.

The only thing I'd gained in my non-career was weight.

Perhaps it wasn't the only thing, I thought, as I plowed my way through one of the semi-edible meals that SAA serves up to passengers who only earn enough money to fly economy class. I didn't have a certificate to prove it, but I'd gained more than waitressing skills during my stint at the Coachman. It wasn't an upmarket pub. Fortunately for my future, the official chef was more jovial than competent. His customers were locals rather than tourists so they were tolerant when their host drank more than they did. He had a tendency to flounder when the pub was busy. And I'd grown up with a mother who specialised in kitchen floundering.

"I'll do this, Pete," I would say briskly as a plume of smoke snaked into the air from the steak charring on the griddle. He started to trust my judgement as I dripped wine and herbs into a casserole he'd overlooked. I had a miscellany of ways to rescue a risotto. I did all the cooking in our London flat. Julia and Mary both had proper jobs so it seemed reasonable for me to take on the catering. I could work miracles with a can of tuna and half a dozen eggs.

But no one mentioned these skills to the Home Office. They stamped APPLICATION DENIED in bold red ink across the page. It was unfair. I brooded sullenly as I tried to wedge a pillow in behind my neck. I hadn't stolen anything for two years. Maybe I thought the London bobbies were more likely to arrest me than the South African police. Or maybe I made a point of avoiding the under-wear section when I went shopping. I could hardly bear to look at g-strings that Mary left draped out to dry in our communal bathroom. London made me even larger than before. We drank a lot of beer at the Coachman. I was now too large for an economy-class seat on SAA.

It was a long flight. Disconnected thoughts tumbled as I tried desperately to fall asleep.

When shall we three meet again? The opening line of Macbeth had evolved into an in-house joke for Mary, Julia and me when we said our various hellos and goodbyes in the years after we left school. We'd said it again at Heathrow before my flight was called.

I'm something of a specialist in opening lines. A few of my mother's genes must be embedded on the fringe of my DNA. Slivers of poems we read at school filter back at times. *When I'm an old woman, I shall wear purple* sounds like something my mother would say.

I remembered another line. *They fuck you up, your mum and dad.* I blamed my luckless mother all the way back to Cape Town because she didn't insist on a career which might have earned me a visa.

➤

THIRTEEN

I'm not sure that I trust hindsight. Or limbo.

A slice of time, after my return from London, falls into both those categories. We were already three years into the new millennium by then. I've loaded innocuous incidents which took place that time with a significance they don't deserve as I've sifted back through a jumble of days that seemed to lack direction. Were there things I should have noticed? Incidents I should have valued more? Did I miss some pointers to the future lurking in the wings?

In retrospect, the three months I spent looking for a job in Cape Town formed a bridge between the past and the present for my mother and me: our roles started to reverse after that. Neither of us could have anticipated that my name would become as semi-famous as hers, that my non-career would outstrip both Julia's and Mary's. I probably outshone them both in sexual adventure, but none of us expected that I would evolve into a mother without ever falling pregnant.

Alzheimer's was a foreign language while we were in limbo. My mother wasn't officially ill and my brother and I weren't officially employed because we both had visa issues. Mine had expired in London, and Karl was waiting for his to be approved in the States. Visas are a great impediment to travel for those as lacking in marketable skills as we were. Karl had dabbled with game ranging in his patchwork past, but it didn't open a lot of doors at the American consulate. He worked a three-month stint at Ulusaba in the Kruger Park before heading off to the States to find Pocahontas and her raffia mats. Karl was always surfing the Net for short term vacancies. He never signed a long-term contract in case something more exciting came up.

My mother still believed in seizing life by the horns at that stage. She insisted that we take advantage of our short-term connection to the luxuries of Ulusaba, particularly as my post-London spirits were so low.

"We've lived in Africa all our lives, but neither of us has ever seen a lion!" she pointed out with gusto. "Not even in a zoo!"

You get special weekend rates at Ulusaba if you're related to a ranger. I protested that I was busy looking for a job, but she swept aside my reservations when she found a special offer on a low price airline.

"Book us in!" she instructed Karl. "We'll never get another chance! Perhaps you can set your sister up with a ranger..."

She wanted to buy an outfit with a safari flavor to mark her prospective viewing of the big five so we headed off to see what Cape Union had to offer for the occasion.

"Any luck?" I asked when she emerged from the changing room.

"I'm going to take this one," said my mother, looking down at the brand name khaki outfit she had bundled in her arms. "It smacks of David Livingstone. And look at this hat!" She looked as if she belonged on the banks of the Zambezi in her wide-brimmed headgear. I nodded approvingly as we made our way to the till. I got a better look at the outfit as she laid her prospective purchase down on the counter.

"Mom," I said in amazement. "How can this possibly fit you? It's Size 32!"

"Is it?" said my mother vaguely. "What size do I take?"

"You daft old bat, "I said fondly as I put it back on the hanger. "When did you move onto another planet? You're either losing your sight or your mind. You couldn't have tried this on!"

"I was concentrating on the hat," she said defensively as we picked out a more capacious outfit. She insisted on wearing the hat to lunch. I didn't give the Size 32 outfit another thought at the time. My mother's been a daft old bat for as long as I can remember so eccentric behaviour wasn't out of character. But a Size 32 seems offbeat when I think about it now. It would have fitted Julia. Why would someone the size of my mother ever have taken it off the shelf?

Was it a glimpse of a lack of perspective which would become increasingly familiar?

➤

Rock Lodge is perched on a koppie with a panoramic view of the lowveld. There were guests sipping champagne in slim, iced glasses on a wooden deck overlooking a dam where a few elephant had cooperatively meandered down to drink. The overflow from the lodge pool cascaded over granite boulders interlaced with trees and ferns.

Karl had met us and the other weekend guests at the airstrip, along with a squad of fellow rangers. They looked better in their khaki than a knight in shining armor. They all looked a bit like Karl: Camel Man material with tanned faces and sun-bleached hair. Their bodies didn't look too shabby either.

"My God, Hannah," whispered my mother surreptitiously out of the corner of her mouth.

"This lot look better than the Big Five. I'd choose a ranger over a lion any day!"

"Don't get your hopes up," I warned her. "It's probably against company policy to seduce a guest."

"I'm not that ambitious," she assured me. "I haven't been seduced by anyone for about a decade. I'll feel successful if none of them call me grandma! But you could give it a try – I'm prepared to settle for a vicarious seduction, now that sixty is on the horizon."

"All seductions are off," I told her. "Remember, we're sharing a room. I'm not forking out all this money for one of us to spend the night in the bathroom while the other one gets lucky next door. Focus on the food. And the animals. Game rangers and German tourists are out of bounds this week."

It was easy to shelve a touch of promiscuity with so many other diversions on hand. We were delighted with our suite. Opulent beds framed by draped mosquito nets. Ochre walls aglow with paintings of tribal people in traditional dress. Wooden artifacts. Woven cushions in warm earthy colors. My mother was particularly taken with the huge brass bath. She loves a nice hot bath. She must have been the cleanest person in Mpumalanga by the time we left. Her bathing fetish nearly made us miss the lions.

I'd strolled up early to have a look around the lodge before we set on our scheduled game drive for sundowners in the wild outdoors. I was engaged in some futile flirting with a particularly attractive ranger when Karl interrupted. "Where's Mom?" he demanded. "It's time to get on the Land Rover."

"Wait!" I pleaded beseechingly as the more punctual guests climbed into their seats. "She must have gotten lost! Please wait!" The Germans were looking pretty hostile as I galloped off to our suite. I flung open the door. The room was empty.

"Oh my God!" I cried. "Where is she?" And then I heard a ripple of water from the bathroom. I peered in to see my mother, lolling like Cleopatra in the tub.

"Hannah!" she smiled. "This is so divine! I've been in here for hours!"

"Get out! "I yelled. "The game drive! What about the

game drive? Karl's waiting on the Land Rover!"

"The game drive?"

"You can't have forgotten the fucking game drive!" I yelled. "Get out! Get dressed!"

I hauled her out of the tub along with what seemed like half the bath water. She's a large woman so this was no easy task. It didn't become any easier in the future, even when her illness made her lose all the weight she'd spent so much time trying to discard when she was healthy. I couldn't inject her with the required urgency. I pity the luckless maid who had to clean up after us when she made her nightly call to turn the bedcovers back and put the chocolates on our pillows. I'd discarded towels and tracksuits and socks in damp piles all over the floor as I tried to force my mom into her clothes and takkies.

"I'm not dry," she complained as I hauled her down the corridor at a gallop that would have made us winners in the English Derby. "I'm going to catch pneumonia on an open truck!"

"You're going to start a third world war if we don't get there soon!" I told her. "Those Germans were already muttering when I left..."

But the Land Rover was still there. Karl had diverted the Germans with a talk about the birds which had fortuitously collected on some nearby branches. My mother was charmingly apologetic as she wedged her large bottom in beside some luckless German. A grey loerie sounded its familiar cry and a discord of hadedahs flew overhead in formation to herald our departure.

I soon forgot that I was furious with my mother. The sun was fading and the trees were etched against the sky. I was amazed to find that Karl knew all their names – Bushveld teak, false marula, weeping bushwillow. Tiny cream flowers hung suspended from the knob-thorn branches. The first rains had already fallen – the trees had donned their summer outfits, decked out for the tourists in subtle shades of green. We caught our breath as Karl steered us offroad, past three kudu cows, their large ears alert and attentive. We passed giraffe, grazing on tree tips. Karl pointed out the red-billed oxpeckers, dotted on their necks like parasites.

"They eat seven thousand ticks a day," he told us.

"How can you possibly know that?" asked my mother aggressively. "You're making it up to impress the Germans!" I nudged her to shut up.

We felt a long way from Cape Town when we stopped for sundowners in the veld – snacks and icy drinks as the sun slipped below the horizon. The stars came out to stud the sky like glowworms. My mother squeezed my hand as we set off again into the gathering darkness. The bush felt different now that it was nighttime. Our other senses seemed to step up a gear to compensate for the lack of sight. Our tracker held a powerful spotlight that moved in an arc through the darkness. Everyone fell silent as we passed shadows that translated into rhino or eland. Eyeball to eyeball with elephant, grazing relentlessly. The spotlight picked out a silent owl, motionless on a gnarled branch.

The radio cackled. ""Ingwe! Ingwe!"

Karl steered our Land Rover through the bush to join the team who'd made the sighting – a leopard at the foot of a tree trunk, disdainful of all the attention. Dappled with dark rosettes but pale in the light that framed her. Her eyes were yellow and alert. She looked lethal.

"I'll remember this forever, Hannah," breathed my mother.

But she didn't. She didn't write a feature on our introduction to game reserves. The most recent memories are the first to go. None of us had any idea what was taking place inside her brain.

We'd become good friends with the Germans by the time we finished supper in the boma that evening. We'd downed several bottles of wine while a group of local Shangaan women sang and danced their way through a ritual dance, their voices raw and ethnic. We joined our new German mates for breakfast the next morning and started reminiscing about the rare sighting of a leopard we'd seen the night before.

"What leopard?" said my mother, and we all laughed. We presumed she was talking about the effects of our heavy night around the campfire. And maybe that's all she was doing.

That's what I mean about the danger of hindsight. I've rethought our stay in Ulusaba in the same way as I reassessed my midnight call from Julia in London. There are three things that bother me about Ulusaba. The Size 32 David Livingstone outfit. Lying in the bath at the start of the game drive. And her remark about the leopard.

I should have asked her what she meant, but I couldn't trust her answers by the time the questions occurred to me.

FOURTEEN

The reason I was in limbo after my return from London was that getting a job in Cape Town wasn't as easy as I thought it would be. I never thought I'd miss the tube, but it certainly made getting from A to B a lot simpler than it was in Cape Town. I'd sold my car before I left for London. Public transport was sadly lacking, especially with my midnight hours. I was forced to move back to Pepper Street with my mother. What self-respecting adult still lives with her mother?

"I'm such a cock-up!" I wept on my mother's ample shoulder. "And I'm a fat cock-up which is the worst kind of cock-up you can be!"

"My darling girl," she protested. "That's nonsense! I'd sell my soul to be as young and sexy as you. You're going through an intercontinental slump. Prolonged jet lag. Part of it's because you've come back home. It seems like a step backward after two years away. It's natural that you're going to miss living with Julia and Mary. It'll take you a while to get your old circle up and running, but you'll find a job. And a place of your own."

She didn't say that I'd find a boyfriend because she knew that would make me cry even more. She knew that I wanted a boyfriend more than I wanted a job. She was still the official mother in our family at that stage, the one who made everything all right again.

Her first suggestion involved a new wardrobe. We started off at Woolies, purely out of habit. My mother had been buying beige underwear there for decades. I suppose it's unrealistic to petition for a block out ban on change room mirrors, but someone should explain to the marketing manager that sales would rise if customers were shielded from direct confrontation with their defects. Even my mother couldn't deny that I looked progressively more awful in each new number I tried. When did my bum reach those dimensions? Were those folds of flesh in the stomach arena? When did ripple become a thigh-related verb? We left empty handed, my gloom deeper than ever.

"We can fix this situation," my mother told me briskly over a recuperation cappuccino. She'd just been commissioned by *Fair Lady* to write a feature on online dating, so she was more solvent than usual. With her signature failure to save money for a rainy day, she booked me in for a week at the spa on a program. It targeted cellulite specifically.

I packed my bags with marked reluctance. I didn't

have the courage to conceal an entire carrot cake at the bottom of my suitcase, but I sneaked in a couple of Kit Kats. I'd heard all about the lettuce regime prevailing at the health farm.

I identified two distinct groups of "inmates" when we took our places at the orientation session. One was focused on maintaining the perfection that had already been achieved. All members of this group were lithe and tanned with fully functional bodies. Their hair was sleek and highlighted. They knew how to work all the machines in the gym. Changing booths held no fears for Group A inmates. I gravitated towards the losers in Group B. I could see they had a cellulite crisis similar to my own.

"We are integral thinkers," the instructor assured us in her opening pep talk. "We feel the need to bring ourselves fully into the experience of life. Expressing ourselves in mind, body, soul and spirit will bring us the personal growth we seek together."

I had no idea what she meant. My spirits sank still further when I answered my wake-up call the following morning. Sally Sunshine was at the door with our early morning beverage.

"Fuck this!" I muttered as I took a tentative sip. It was Epsom salts. The next morning it was parsley tea. Lunch and supper did little to improve our spirits. Day one featured lettuce, cucumber and two almonds. There was also a carrot. I dreamed of the cake at the Seattle Coffee shop as I stoically munched my way through it.

I felt positively faint when we presented ourselves at

the gym. Time ground to a halt on the treadmill. After what seemed like an eternity, I sneaked a glance at the clock. Thirty-one seconds had passed. I couldn't believe it. The machine was obviously malfunctioning. I gave it a furtive kick to hurry it along. This was a mistake. I lost my footing and fell off in a loud disruptive manner. I slunk off to the sauna.

But I phoned my mother in triumph after the final weigh-in! Several kilograms had vanished! They could hardly pry me off the scale.

>

"And now for Plan B!" purred my mother who'd been busy researching her online dating feature. "The best way to find out is to try it ourselves," she assured me. She was always game to give everything a try, while she was still the mother I'd grown up with. It's hard to believe how risk-aversive she became as her illness took hold.

We giggled like schoolgirls as we settled down to work on our profiles after registering for MWEB's online dating. *Intelligent woman seeks interesting companion* was my mother's bait. I decided on *Sexy Dolores eager for company*. I was sick of being Hannah.

"I've got seven new messages!" yelled my mother triumphantly. Sexy Dolores had even more. My favorite called himself *Monsieur Cool*. Subtitled *A really naughty boy*. Followed by at least seven exclamation marks. He claimed to be a raconteur of note with an interest in a feisty sensual partner. He admitted to a totally dysfunctional family and ticked at least eighteen different musical genres as his favorite. I thought I'd give him a try when I got to his fondness for martial arts.

"Listen to this one," said my mother as she browsed hopefully through her replies. *Scorpio*. Subtitled *One Foot in the Cape*. We liked his face and the touch of grey at his temples. He claimed to have a sophisticated sense of humor and isolated jazz as his musical favorite.

"He sounds just your type!" I enthused. We felt a surge of hope as we took a deep breath and sent off our respective applications to Monsieur Cool and Scorpio.

"Monsieur Cool can't spell!" said my mother scathingly when she read his response. Spelling isn't my strongest point either so that didn't put me off. He'd included a photo with his latest email. He was muscular with a rather racy tattoo. Scorpio sounded terribly excited when he found out that my mother was Chloe Cartwright. He set up a lunch to precede an afternoon at duplicate bridge at the Western Province Bridge Club in Green Point. My mother had listed bridge as one of her interests in her introductory letter.

"But you can't play bridge!" I protested when I read his plans for their inaugural afternoon.

My mother looked offended. "Don't be ridiculous!" she protested haughtily. "I've been playing bridge every Thursday evening for the last two decades!" This was true. There was a gang of about six of my mother's closest friends who rotated on the bridge roster every Thursday evening. They called themselves The Inner Circle. They always played at our house because the others liked to take a break from domestic duties such as making supper and supervising homework. My mother had just as many kids as the rest of them, but our regime excluded supper and homework.

They didn't play much bridge in the Inner Circle from what Karl and I could hear as we lounged around watching TV while they pretended to be playing. I'm not even certain they knew how to score. Karl and I used to moan about the racket as they shrieked with laughter and waltzed through to the kitchen to get another bottle of wine out of the fridge.

"I think duplicate bridge at the Western Province Bridge Club will have a higher profile than bridge on Thursday evenings with the Inner Circle," I warned her. But she ignored me. She washed her hair and got all tarted up for the occasion. She introduced me to Scorpio when he arrived to fetch her. I must say he was very attractive. He seemed delighted to meet an author of such high renown. Maybe I was worrying unnecessarily, I thought.

My mother looked as if she'd just survived a suicide bomb in Iraq when she limped in that evening. Scorpio dropped her off on the road. He didn't even walk her to the door.

"Get me a drink!" she said weakly as she collapsed into her favorite chair.

"I was cold with fear by the time we got there," she told me as she sipped a reviving scotch and soda. "He wasn't even vaguely interested in talking about my books at lunch time. He kept asking me what conventions I played."

Scorpio had made the fatal assumption that an academic like my mother would also be a competent bridge player. There was a tournament director stalking down the aisles, on the alert for foul play or malpractice. She couldn't very well get under the table and hide so she picked up her hand and started playing.

"My God!" she said. "The afternoon got progressively more dreadful. Some of the people there would make Attila the Hun look tame and inoffensive. "Call the tournament director!" they yelled whenever I made a suspect bid. I thought they were going to summon the police and throw me into jail."

We never saw Scorpio again. We hoped I'd have better luck with Monsieur Cool. I tried on about ten different outfits before our assignation. I couldn't decide on my priorities. Slim or sexy?

"Go for sexy," advised my mother. "You've billed yourself as *Sexy Dolores*. You can hardly arrive in a nun's habit."

A short black number got the nod. I smiled approvingly at my reflection in the glass and set out with a spring in my step and hope in my heart.

I was early. I'd have a clear view of Monsieur Cool when he walked up to the wine bar. I'd made contingency plans to fade into the darkness if he didn't look as appealing as he had in his photograph. Thank God I had the foresight not to include a photo of myself. He wouldn't know I was Dolores, even if he caught a glimpse of me lurking in the shadows.

And then, my God, it's him! I recognized him as soon as he got out of the car. Taller than I expected, casually dressed in denims and a brand name jacket. Both his tattoo and muscles were out of sight. I hoped I'd get to see both as the evening progressed. I ran a brush through my hair and took a deep breath and strode with confidence en route what my destiny.

I summoned up my most flirtatious smile as I slipped into the seat beside him at the bar.

"Monsieur Cool?" I purred. I preened as his eyes slid over me from top to toe. There was a tangible silence.

"Christ!" he said in obvious disbelief. "You're Dolores?"

He slammed a barely sipped drink onto the bar counter. My hands were trembling as I watched him stride towards the door and slam it closed behind him.

My mother was very supportive after my online dating rejection. She didn't put me on a diet or nag about me lounging around and getting in her way. She fed me carrot cake from the corner store and made me nice hot cups of tea in the middle of the night when I couldn't sleep and she was busy writing.

I stopped feeling so miserable when I read emails from Julia and Mary complaining about the London weather. I saw the advert for a waitress in the window at Gabrielle's. I knew Max liked me when I went for the interview.

"This is the start of a winning decade for you, my darling," my mother assured me as I forced myself into my new Gabrielle's T-shirt and set off to take my first orders.

We were both optimistic, but I don't think even she could have predicted how bright my future would be.

Nor the bleakness of hers.

I couldn't help remembering how we'd laughed about the Scorpio fiasco when one of the stalwarts of The Inner Circle phoned me in voice laced with concern. My mother couldn't remember why they were there when they arrived for their regular bridge date one Thursday evening.

FIFTEEN

The initial drawcard of Gabrielle's was its location on the corner of Pepper and Long Streets. It was only a few blocks from our house which is a major plus if you just got back from London without a car. I missed London. Buildings in Cape Town don't date back for centuries. Long Street feels old by Cape Town standards because the buildings are Victorian. I love the lacy, cast-iron balconies above shops that sell everything from books to antiques and funky clothing. The little galleries opening out into the street are somehow not incongruous, tucked in beside porn shops and internet cafes. There's a buzz on Long Street. Casually dressed people browse around or queue to get into a club or jazz bar. Vendors ply you with food and flowers. Or drugs. You can get anything you want on Long Street.

Gabrielle's had become a landmark over the first decade of the millennium. It started off as shabby old house which Max Osinsky snapped up as a long-term investment in the late eighties, before Long Street became as fashionable as it is today. Max has been in property for decades so he was good at spotting a sound investment. He stripped the floors and painted the rooms and fitted out the kitchen. He hired a jazz singer with a saxophone and a smoky voice. He also hired Daniel.

Daniel was much higher than me in the food chain at Gabrielle's at the outset of our peculiar relationship. He was already the chief chef when Max signed me on as a lowly waitress. He'd won several awards.

"And this is Daniel," said Max, sounding as if he was showing me one of the crown jewels as he took me on the rounds of my new colleagues. I can't say there was a burst of electricity as Daniel and I shook hands and smiled our obligatory smiles, but I remember thinking that he might merit a second glance. And Daniel always gave women a second glance. It was part of his persona.

I've never been to France so I don't really have any idea what the average Frenchman looks like, but Daniel fits the Gallic stereotype I've picked up from magazines and movies. He's a compact man, his ebony skin dark against the whiteness of his chef's uniform. His face is lean and alert, his voice warm, slightly accented. His family still speak French at home. He's very attractive. He'd look at home in a Paris attic, daubing paint onto an easel.

He was certainly an artist in the culinary line which explains why he could do no wrong in Max's eyes. Gabrielle's boasted a mouth-watering list of specials that Daniel changed every evening. Grilled baby kingklip rolled in macadamia nuts, drizzled in mango and mampoer sauce. Kudu medallions, wrapped in bacon with marula jelly. Paper-thin ostrich carpaccio. Avocado with ginger and honey. His presentation gave the already-delicious food an extra dimension. A sprig of fresh herbs. A swirl of sauce. I wanted to try a mouthful of every dish I put down in front of a customer, some of whom had driven over from the northern suburbs or the Atlantic seaboard for a special occasion.

The waitresses loved Daniel. So did the customers. His social skills were almost as much of a trademark as his cooking. He came out of the kitchen and circulated between the tables. His accent gave him a head start with women. My mother adored him from the outset. She dreamed of confetti and a wedding banquet. She thought being a mother-in-law might provide her with a plot for her next novel.

>~

Daniel's the only South-African-born son of the Mbu family who made their way down to Cape Town as refugees after one of the episodes of violence that have torn the Congo apart during a turbulent century. They shrugged off colonial rule by France and England more violently in the Congo than we did in South Africa. It helps if you have Mandela in your political line-up. Talking of South African politicians, I've always thought that Daniel's father looks a bit like Mbeki. He's also small with a neat grey beard but I think his blood is warmer. The Mbu family ethos is as sociable as the Cartwright's which is why our families have slotted into place like the missing pieces on a jig-saw.

This was particularly thanks to my mother. She was much more at home in Khayelitsha than Julia's mother would have been. She's been involved with the municipal library there ever since the government decided to build the township. Karl and I had been carted off to the townships, even as kids. We could sing the struggle songs as lustily as anyone else in the crowd at a political rally. We couldn't speak Xhosa, but that didn't matter with the Mbus because they spoke French. And English. They were a trilingual family. The Congo was a multilingual country with a sound educational basis, thanks to the efforts of the Catholic church. The Mbus were Catholic. And they were all talkative. I felt as if I'd been to Brazzaville myself as I got to know them, listened to their stories.

Their particular crisis was in the sixties. The stories were so long and involved that I got muddled over the details. I remember a massacre at Stanleyville. Mobutu and Lumumbo. I'm not sure how to spell their names, but I know a multitude was slaughtered by the army of one or the other. I'm not sure who won, but I know that Daniel's family was on the losing side. Along with thousands of others, they streamed out of the country with their belongings on their backs and made their arduous way to Cape Town which was as far as you can get from Brazzaville without jumping into the sea.

Daniel's father told me he had to swallow his pride

when they got here. He used to sigh when he reminisced about the past, as old people are wont to do on the least provocation.

"It's hard to move away from your roots, Hannah," he told me. "In Brazzaville, I had a name. People knew me." His restaurant was called Le Jardin. It was mentioned in tourist brochures before the rebels tore them up and threw them into the sea. I'm no history scholar, but I know that Brazzaville wasn't segregated like Cape Town in the sixties. There may have been a few curfews, but there were no laws to stop Daniel's father owning an up-market restaurant. Le Jardin sounded like a Congolese version of Gabrielle's. He had to move back to the bottom of the culinary tree when he arrived in Cape Town, desperate to support his wife and family. He sighed a lot during that story too.

"No one would employ a black chef," he complained. "I was back to chopping and slicing when I started work in Greenpoint. I had to catch a bus and two taxis to get there." He said it took him hours every day to make his way from the ramshackle home he'd set up beside his fellow refugees in a shelter sponsored by the Catholic church in Mowbray. Those refugees were a small squad of French speakers, bound by their language and their distance from home. The future looked bleak, but he worked his way back to solvency. The Mbus didn't live in a ramshackle house by the time Daniel was born.

By the time he left school in the early nineties, it was an advantage to be black in the hospitality industry. Tourism in Cape Town was booming, and Daniel had food and cooking in his bloodstream. He was a natural for selection when Southern Sun opened up its training program. After a two-year stint on the Paris circuit, he could virtually choose his kitchen on his return. Daniel's skills turned Gabrielle's into a long-term winner.

➤

I slotted in well with the staff at Gabrielle's, though Daniel soon became my favorite. He fancied me too. It was my culinary skills that tipped the balance in my favor. I'd picked them up from my surrogate mothers while I was growing up. The pickings in the orange side of the house in Pepper Street were so frugal that there was never anything appetizing to eat unless I cooked it myself. I spent hours in the kitchen with both Fatima and Julia's mom while my own mother was out on her Khayelitsha beat, starting libraries or campaigning for the franchise.

Both of my surrogate mothers were delighted to find an acolyte in their kitchens. I learned the cooking of Provence from one and the traditional dishes of Cape Town from the other. Fatima didn't have a daughter and Julia's domestic skills were zero. She had an appetite like a sparrow so food was irrelevant to her. I was like a carthorse in comparison. My mother was delighted to sponsor my burgeoning interest in stove-related activities which were so alien to her. Karl would drive me to Hout Bay to buy fresh fish from the local boats while he jogged up Chapman's Peak to get fit for rugby. I sifted through fresh vegetables and herbs at our corner store. I may have lacked Daniel's formal training, but I had a flair for food.

It wasn't as easy to make my mark at Gabrielle's as it had been at the Coachman in London. Waitresses couldn't masquerade as sous chefs under Daniel's regime. He had his finger in every pie in the kitchen. But the human factor always plays a part, even in an operation as smoothly run as Gabrielle's. Their official sous chef had graduated at the top of her class at the hotel school in Granger Bay, but it turned out that she couldn't make babies as well as she made puff pastry. She and her partner were desperate to fall pregnant. She told me all about her fertility specialist. She walked around the kitchen, armed with a thermometer, but she wasn't interested in how rare the fillet was. She needed to know when she was ovulating. She had to hang up her apron and rush out to a sexual rendezvous whenever it happened. She never told me where they met up. Maybe they were at it like rabbits in carparks all over Cape Town.

It provided me with a number of wonderful opportunities to step into the breach at a moment's notice. Daniel came to rely on my opinion when he launched the special for the week. It wasn't long before he became eager to explore more than my taste buds.

"Don't drop my work of art, Hannah," he'd whisper, nibbling the back of my neck as I bent down at the counter to pick up my orders. I was much less likely to drop the plates than I was to eat everything on them before they got to the person who'd placed the order. I loved Daniel's cooking. I gobbled up the leftovers like a stray mongrel, nosing for scraps in the dustbin. I ate far too much rich food for my own good. That was what caused the problem with Daniel when he tried to persuade me to go out with him on a date.

"I can't possibly go out with you, Daniel," I told him emphatically when he raised the issue over a bottle of wine that we'd opened when the last guests had left one evening, about six months after I'd started working at Gabrielle's. "It's a matter of principle," I explained, beginning to slur my words as the wine level in the bottle diminished.

"What principle?" asked Daniel, disbelievingly. He'd seen me being collected by Tom, Dick or Harry, almost on a rotation basis. I clearly wasn't involved in a deep and lasting relationship that might preclude a night on the tiles with the chef.

"You're smaller than me," I told him as I slugged back another glass of house wine. "I never go out with anyone who's smaller than me."

"I'm not smaller than you," protested Daniel, dragging me to my feet and standing me beside him at the wall. "Look," he pointed. "We're exactly on the same level."

"It's not a height issue," I told him drunkenly. "It's width. I'm twice as wide as you! Look at your skinny little legs. They make mine look like a baobab in the lowveld!"

"I love your legs," purred Daniel, sliding his hand up my thigh.

"No, Daniel!" I protested firmly. "You're disqualified. I have very strict width criteria and you just don't measure up. I don't feel feminine when I'm with a thin man. I feel vulnerable."

Daniel was undeterred. His hand resumed its passage up my thigh. It seemed a good idea to help him when it came to buttons. And zips. I had some reservations about his penis when I reached it. It looked almost as insubstantial as his skinny little legs.

"I thought black men were supposed to be hung like stallions," I told him, stroking with reassuring fingers.

"Don't underestimate it," he warned me. "It's a precision instrument. Like a Swiss watch," he bragged.

"Are my breasts too big?" I whispered anxiously.

"Not at all," he told me on close inspection. "You have amazing breasts. And thighs," he added approvingly as we kissed and licked and became more intimately acquainted.

"I love your skin," I told him. Daniel was much blacker than the average South African man. His skin was dark and smooth. I found the contrast between our tangled limbs a real turn-on. Very erotic. Ebony and ivory. We could have been the inspiration behind John Lennon's famous song. Or maybe it was Paul McCartney who wrote it. Temperatures had risen so high by then that I could hardly remember how to breathe, let alone worry about the Beatles.

Because that's when Daniel played the multiple orgasm card. A single orgasm was already a major incentive for me when it came to sex with Tom, Dick and Harry, but it was Daniel who delivered the multiple variety. It was – well, multiple, I suppose. A poet would probably choose a word like sublime, but I didn't brag, even to Julia and Mary. Multiple orgasms are a private affair. We used up quite a bit of energy every time I had one, but unfortunately it didn't make me any thinner.

Daniel didn't meet my criteria for a boyfriend, much as I liked him. He became a human version of my secret drawer. I didn't tell anyone about my multiple orgasms with the chef, even though I came to rely on them to boost my morale when I was feeling down.

SIXTEEN

Daniel became my closest friend while Julia and Mary were in London. We saw each other virtually every day at work. He'd evolved from a township boy into a black diamond and Max paid him a lot of money. He still had strong township roots, but he bought a house in Gardens because he didn't want the daunting journey to work that his father had to make. He couldn't buy a fashionable loft in Greenpoint because he had Jezebel and Lucifer to consider.

They weren't rivals of mine. One of the things I found most attractive about Daniel were his dogs. They were almost as appealing as the orgasms. We had never had a dog in Pepper Street so I knew nothing about the charm of warm fur and pink tongues until I was introduced to Jez and little Luce. I was enslaved from our first meeting.

I learned that they were two of the devil's closest henchman. Jezebel was a bouvier – an unstoppable woollen tsunami, only more dangerous. She ate up bed-spreads and groceries with equal relish. She was a very pretty dog. Daniel and I loved Jez. She slept on our bed every night which didn't leave much room for either sex or slumber. Lucifer was her spaniel consort, a hound of enormous charm. Black as Hades with jaunty golden eyebrows. Her ears and paws were streaked with gold. Only the vet thought she was a mongrel. Her spot was between our pillows.

It felt as if I was living in Noah's ark when I moved in with Daniel at the end of 2004. Our relationship was about a year old by then. Time passed quickly, running a restaurant.

Because we worked together – and because Daniel was the boss – we were able to synchronize our shifts so that we had off-duty time together. We valued time at home with the dogs at the Gardens house. Daniel had built up a great selection of CDs. We lounged on the couch, buried in snuggling dogs, listening to jazz. We cooked for each other. There is something very sensual about cream. Drizzled chocolate. We sipped wine from long-stemmed glasses. We nuzzled each other, along with the dogs. We told each other all our highs and lows. We gossiped about the staff and the people we dated. His was the ear I confided in as my mother became increasingly irritating. We were a great comfort to each other as our non-relationship drifted nowhere in the years that followed.

><

Daniel was exposed to my mother's shortcomings when he decided to have his house repainted. The problem with painting a house is that it's so invasive. They move out all the furniture and there are ladders and newspapers and workmen everywhere. The whole situation becomes completely untenable when you add a couple of ill-disciplined dogs to the equation. They barked insanely when they were introduced to the painter and his team. We knew they would stop at nothing in their efforts to eat one of them.

"They'll have to go into kennels," said Daniel sadly. The girls had never been in a kennel. We thought they might eat the other inmates.

"I know!" I cried, struck with my own brilliance. "They can stay with me at my mother's! She adores them! I'll move back home until the painters go. They might be nervous in a new home."

I must say, they didn't appear to be nervous when I drove them over to Pepper Street and unloaded them and their baskets from the car. The girls nearly knocked my mother over as I opened the door.

"Dear God!" she gasped as she struggled to regain her balance. "How long did you say they're staying?"

"Jezebel! Lucifer!" I yelled ineffectually. We watched them climb the walls and strum out a tune on the piano. "They'll settle down in a moment," I assured her. "They're just finding their feet." They found a lot more than their feet during the duration of the visit which dragged on seemingly forever, as anything to do with contractors tends to do. Their crime rate was as high as Joburg's. They did more damage than a gang in the Cape Flats as they dug up plants and dismembered cushions in the lounge.

"They're usually so well behaved," I lied. Fortunately, my mother has low standards when it comes to house-keeping. She doesn't own any Persian rugs or leather shoes so the damage to property wasn't catastrophic. She was quite sanguine when she found her couch and bed covered with dog hair. She adored the girls. My mother and I actually look a bit like bouviers ourselves, with our family mane of hair and our substantial dimensions. Perhaps that's why Daniel loved us.

But my mother was getting so bloody forgetful. She claims she forgot the dogs were staying with her which seems impossible to believe. I always sleep late after I get home from a shift, and they were sleeping on my bed. Out of sight. She said she didn't notice Lucifer had slipped out when she opened the kitchen door and drove off to an early meeting. The next thing I knew was when she exploded into my bedroom in a state of uncontrolled hysteria.

"I've killed Luce!" she screamed. "I was reversing out the gate when I heard this dreadful thunk! She's lying in the drive! I think she's dead!"

I nearly knocked her over as I hurtled out of the door. It was true! The dearest spaniel in world was lying in the drive! Her bouvier sister bounded all over my mother and me as we knelt down beside the corpse, weeping and wailing like the rivers of Babylon. And then Lucifer opened her eyes.

"She's alive!" I screamed. "Get the keys! We've got to get her to the vet!"

The adrenaline was pumping as I cradled her in my arms. Tears streamed down my face as I heard her whimper. She cried even more when I picked her up.

"I'm so sorry, darling dog," whispered my luckless mother. I laid little Lucifer on her lap as carefully as the crown jewels. Jezebel was terribly excited at the prospect of a morning drive and leapt into the back seat. She barked joyously all the way to the vet. I nearly stalled as I revved the engine in my haste to get away. I sped off without closing the gate which was good news for a passing thief who strolled in and rode off on Daniel's new mountain bike. We'd moved it over to my mother's along with the girls because Daniel was afraid it might get stolen by a painter. News of the stolen bike went down nearly as badly as running over one of the girls.

I exploded into the waiting room with my armful of spaniel. I looked like a freshly drowned Ophelia with my hair on end and my tear-streaked face. I noticed to my alarm that I was still in my pajamas. The receptionists all clucked their tongues and made comforting noises as they shepherded me through to the surgery. It seemed like hours before the vet arrived.

Lucifer lived up to her name. She made an instant recovery the minute he walked in. She was like a soccer star for Man United. One moment she was down and out, whimpering and whining. As soon as the vet touched her, she sat up and wagged her tail. He felt all over for broken bones. Looked in her eyes for evidence of concussion. Not a whimper. She'd recently returned from the parlor. A ribbon was still tied rakishly to one ear. She looked as perky as if she were setting out for the bloody dog-show.

"She seems fine," said the vet.

"But my mother hit her," I insisted. "We thought she was dead! She was in pain! I'm sure she must have some damage somewhere..." I felt so embarrassed that I changed my prayers. I prayed the bloody dog would topple over and die, but God continued to ignore me.

"Obviously just a bit of shock," he said reassuringly, typing the bill for his one-minute consultation into the computer.

We prayed that the painters would soon be finished, but, of course, we live in Cape Town so it started to rain. We knew the girls were at our house until the cold front passed over. I stuck notices on the doors to remind my mother to close them in the interests of our canine guests. I thought she was forgetful because she didn't pay attention.

Maybe that's all it was at that stage.

➤

I've more recent memories of my mother with Daniel and his dogs as she evolved into a different person after I was forced to move back to Pepper Street on a permanent basis. Living with an Alzheimer's patient felt like being on house arrest. Ironically, house arrest of political protesters had been one of the issues my mother had campaigned against during her activist days. I couldn't take her out of the house. Her behavior was so unpredictable that even buying eggs and bread was a potential nightmare. She'd walk beside the trolley, meek as a lamb, but there was always the possibility of a riot when the cashier took the money.

"She's stealing my money!" she'd howl, to the consternation of everyone else in the queue. She tore a two hundred rand note in half when I tried to grab it back from her. It seemed safer to keep her at home. It was Daniel who protested.

"You can't keep her inside like a prisoner," he told me. "There's nothing physically wrong with her. I know she panics at Pick n Pay with the lights and the buzz. Strangers handling her money. But we could try taking her to walk in Cecilia Forest..."

It became a regular outing. Daniel would pull up outside Pepper Street. We'd load my mother into the back seat beside Jezebel and Lucy. God knows why she wasn't as frightened by the dogs as she was by the cashier at Pick n Pay. An assault by fur and paws and pink tongues was enough to terrify anyone but, for some reason, it made her laugh. And she laughed so rarely now. Maybe she remembered that she loved the dogs.

The forestry department was cutting down pine trees on the day that's lodged in my memory. No doubt deforestation is part of some long-term conservation plan, but we felt outraged when we came upon the workmen as we followed our usual shady route through the trees. It looked as if the landscape had suffered a devastating attack. We heard the whine of a saw. There was a moment of stillness as the tree stood stubbornly upright, in defiance of the mortal wound inflicted on its trunk. Almost in slow motion, it toppled and crashed to the ground in a tangle of branches.

My mother began to wail. A thin, high-pitched wail. Despairing. It sounded as if she'd witnessed the end of the world. I couldn't get her to stop. Daniel took her by her shoulders and turned her in the opposite direction. He led her back into the safety of the trees. Her keening gradually died as he sat her down on the edge of a boulder and comforted her. My mind has a snapshot of that moment, filed in my bank of memories. An ochre-and-orange-streaked boulder. A glimpse of blue sky between the foliage. And Daniel, sitting beside my mother with her tear-stained face, his arms dark around her white T-shirt, the dogs clustered at their feet. It's like a treasured family portrait. I'd like to have it framed above the fireplace where I would see it every day.

Her wailing haunted me. She sounded as if her world was as demolished as the forest. It felt like she was mourning everything she'd lost. I couldn't bear it. I was tempted to leave her in the forest. Even when she was still in her right mind, there was a good chance she'd never find her way home.

Maybe she would revert to the wild and forage quietly with the squirrels while I got on with my own life?

>

SEVENTEEN

My mother knew she had Alzheimer's, but as Google told me, denial is common in the early stages. My mother certainly fit the standard profile.

"I'll be fine now that I've started taking these pills," she assured me when I collected the first dose of Aricept from the chemist. Aricept is an international brand name. I didn't trust the generic alternative. Her medical aid didn't cover it which still seems outrageous. Someone should have a word with the person who makes the decisions about what illnesses are kosher. Medical aids are wary of anything that sounds like mental illness, but Alzheimer's is as much of a terminal disease as cancer. Probably more so. They've made a lot of progress with certain forms of cancer. Cervical and prostate cancer can be cured if they're diagnosed in the early stages, but there's no cure for Alzheimer's, however early you pick up the signs.

My mother had a lot more faith in the efficacy of

Aricept than I did. It's supposed to retard the breakdown of the neurotransmitters or whatever it is that needs retarding. I find the medical details confusing, but I noted that Google doesn't claim that Aricept stops anything in its tracks. It doesn't even say it slows the process down. It does slow it for some people, but *some* is not the same as all. As it turned out, my mother wasn't going to be one of the lucky ones.

"She doesn't want me to move back home," I told Karl. "She's still praying that Daniel and I will get married." I'd been living with Daniel for a couple of years by then. Purely for convenience. It had nothing to do with his precision penis. Well, virtually nothing.

"She can't possibly stay on her own," said Karl emphatically. "She'll leave the stove on and the whole house will go up in flames. "You'll have to hire a fulltime maid from Happy Housewives or whatever they call them."

"Marvellous Maids," I corrected wearily. "I've already suggested that but she refuses to have a stranger in the house. I think she's getting a bit paranoid. She seems much less laid back about everything these days."

"Why don't you phone Miriam in the Transkei?" suggested Karl.

"Because she's about ninety," I told him in withering tones. "She's probably also riddled with Alzheimer's. She'd probably help to fan the flames."

"I don't mean Miriam herself. I'm sure she'll have a daughter. Or a cousin. She always had more brothers than Joseph and his technicolor dream-coat," urged Karl.

This was a brilliant idea! My mother was far less hostile to the prospect of Miriam's niece than she'd been about some random stranger. Miriam was almost family. She was upset when I phoned to tell her that my mother was ill, but she just laughed when I told her how forgetful she'd become. She said my mother had always been forgetful. "She's just getting old! Like me!" she laughed.

"But she's only sixty-one, Miriam," I pointed out. "That's not very old. She's definitely sick. The doctor said so."

I could hear that Miriam didn't think the matter was as urgent as I suggested, but she rose to the occasion anyway. She had a niece who wanted to get a job in the big city. Both my mother and I made Dorothy feel very welcome when she arrived on the bus from the Transkei. My mother spoke some Xhosa because of all the time she'd spent in the townships. She seemed more able to remember Xhosa than where she'd put her car keys. Alzheimer's is a strange disease. Even the doctors don't understand it.

I certainly didn't understand it when my mother told me that she was being robbed. Dorothy had been with her for over a year and everything seemed almost hunky dory if you ignored the clothes issue. My mother seemed to be wearing the same clothes every time I called. They were always creased. I suggested that we go shopping when I noticed the stains on the front of her blouse.

"I don't need any clothes," she assured me. Dorothy told me that it was difficult to get my mother to change her clothes, even when she went to bed. Curiouser and curiouser, as Alice said so famously. It felt as if I was also in Wonderland when my mother told me she thought Dorothy was taking her money. She lowered her voice and beckoned me over mysteriously as if we were taking part in a soap opera.

"Twenty rand is missing," she whispered.

"Twenty rand is missing?" I echoed, sounding as if I had Alzheimer's myself. "What do mean? Where is twenty rand missing from, for God's sake?"

"From my wallet," she hissed. "That girl! She's taking my money. Keep your voice down! She listens to everything I say!"

I could hardly believe my ears, not only because I knew Dorothy was such an unlikely thief. What was even more unlikely was the possibility that mother would have any idea how many twenty rand notes she had in her wallet.

"Oh rubbish, Mom!" I said indignantly. "Dorothy would never steal your money!"

"It's gone!" said my mother with finality in her voice. "And it's not only my money. I have to hide other things away from her as well."

Anyone who knows my mother would have been as shocked as I was to hear her say this. Miriam was part of our family. I cringed at the thought of how she would react if she could hear what my mother was saying about her niece. Miriam loved my mother. She loved Karl and me as well. I knew Dorothy would have been handpicked by Miriam to support us when she heard that my mother was sick. It was inconceivable that she would steal my mother's money. Almost as inconceivable as it was that my mother would suspect her.

"It's as if she's turned into a stranger!" I wept to Karl when I phoned to tell him about the latest crisis. Karl's face was creased with worry as I talked to him on Skype through my blur of tears. I must have looked even worse to him because he told me was coming home to judge the situation himself.

I knew how fast she was going downhill when I told her Karl had booked his ticket.

"Karl?" she asked.

That floored me more than the theft allegations about Dorothy. It stopped me in my tracks completely. I put my arms around her and held her like a precious piece of Doulton china. I could never replace her if she broke, but I feared she was already broken when she said Karl's name with a question in her voice.

But it was a good reunion in the end. I was learning that Alzheimer's is an up and down affair. I was terrified that she wouldn't recognize him when he walked out with his rucksack at the airport, but I think Karl's face is safely carved in granite in my mother's memory. I felt a surge of hope as her face lit up like a candle. She sounded completely normal as she called for one of our traditional family hugs. Karl strode towards us, looking more like our dead father than ever. It felt right and familiar, the three of us standing with our arms around each other at Cape Town airport.

My initial surge of hope had subsided by the end

of Karl's two-week visit. Not that there was anything extreme. She didn't take her clothes off and walk down Strand Street in the early morning traffic. She didn't forget who Karl was. In fact, she seemed to take it for granted that he was there. She didn't seem to register that he had flown across the Atlantic Ocean to see her. She didn't even cry when he packed his bags and flew back to Colorado.

"It's as if she thinks I'm just going off to work at the office," said Karl as I drove him to the airport. That alone was enough to make us worried. Karl had never been to an office in his life so that triggered alarm bells all over the building. There was an accumulation of little details which made us anxious. Karl had walked into the kitchen one morning and found her packing a suitcase. She was throwing in tea bags and cheese and dish cloths.

"Jesus, Mom," said Karl. "What are you doing? Where are you going?"

But she didn't know the answers to his questions. She slammed the suitcase shut and tried to lock it. Maybe she thought Karl had joined ranks with Dorothy.

Karl said that he felt that he was leaving me in an active minefield when he went to board his plane. But what can you do? Emigration is a fact of life for lots of families in South Africa. For upper-income families anyway. We'd never felt like an upper-income family but I guess we always qualified, compared to the average family in this country. That's one of the complicated facts of life in Africa. A family in Soweto may be poor, but their family is all around to help them through the bad times.

My mother had a lot of support in terms of friends, but we were rather low on family.

I could understand why Karl suggested that I should move home and look after my mother on a full-time basis.

There was no one else.

EIGHTEEN

Initially, I thought it was a calamity when Max followed the example of other wealthy South Africans who've set up a diaspora all over the planet to be close to their grandchildren in the new global village. Max had two children in Sydney and he decided to join them when he heard that a baby was on the way. The staff and customers were devastated. We all adored Max and Gabrielle's was his brainchild.

"It won't be the same without him," I whined as I sulked in Daniel's comforting arms after Max made the announcement to the staff. I didn't like the sound of the prospective buyer. He had plans to modernise all the facilities. It was going to be bigger. Brasher. "It sounds like a fucking Wimpy!" I sighed despairingly.

"Nothing's final yet," Daniel reminded me as he stroked my arm in what I felt was an inattentive way. I knew he wasn't really listening.

"Maybe I'll put in an offer myself," he mused.

I was astounded. "Where will you suddenly get the money to buy a restaurant?" I asked disbelievingly. "You can't expect Max to give Gabrielle's away for nothing, just because you're friends!"

But Daniel knew more about buying a restaurant than I did. It was one of the courses they'd had to study while he was qualifying. Southern Sun was big into black entrepreneurship in a field where restaurant owners are predominantly white and Indian.

"Buying Gabrielle's will probably cost me less than buying this house," he pointed out. "I'm not buying the property. I'll have to pay rent. All I'm paying for is goodwill and the fittings. The goodwill might be expensive because Gabrielle's is so well established, but the fittings are old. We're always complaining about them. I stand a good chance of getting finance."

Max advised Daniel to use a broker when he approached him with his idea. This sounded like a good idea. I didn't want Daniel to end up in jail after a rash bid of more millions than he had. Max was in the business. He put us in touch with a reputable broker who wouldn't give bad advice. Max and Daniel were already in cahoots as buyer and seller so the broker couldn't play one off against the other.

I went with Daniel when he met the broker. We knew immediately that we were out of our depth so we enlisted Max's accountant to bolster our confidence. This was fortunate. The broker was an assured young man, but he might as well have been talking Russian when he raised the issues we would have to consider. Registering as a CC. An offer to purchase. Application for credit card facilities. Lease approval from the landlord. Due Diligence on the financials.

"What's due diligence?" I asked Daniel when we slunk back to Gabrielle's for a reviving cup of their trademark coffee. I could feel the waters closing in over my head. I was a waitress, for God's sake. I had nothing of value to contribute. I looked down the list of due diligence suggestions that Daniel would have to carry out if the offer were accepted. He was supposed to query the fixed assets and the month end closing stock amount. Medical Aid. Employment contracts. PAYE. Pensions and provident funds. Agreements with service providers. And now there's the whole employment equity to consider. There appeared to be a lot more to running Gabrielle's than merely serving the food.

"I can't possibly go through with this," Daniel told me ruefully. "I'm a chef. I can't be an owner."

"I'll help you," I lied reassuringly. "We can do it together."

And believe it or not, we did. It was much easier than setting up a business from scratch because Gabrielle's was already a going concern. The systems were all in place and producing a positive turnover. We just had to keep things going. The staff all stayed because they loved Daniel. Our darling Max put his grandchild on hold for seven months while he showed us the ropes and pointed out the pitfalls.

Daniel and I had more business flair than either of us expected. My mother bragged to her book-club and her bridge circle. I felt like e-mailing a copy of the returns for our first financial year to my headmistress who'd been so discouraging about my future prospects. It was exciting to have a proper job! Every night I said a grateful prayer to any gods who were listening before I switched off the lights and snuggled in beside Daniel.

➤

Daniel and I became even more of a team when we were chosen to host M-Net's new version of a food show. *Daniel and Hannah* was a lucky break for us, so soon after Daniel launched out on his own. The whole country was coming up with new initiatives to coincide with the World Cup. My role may have been less elevated than Daniel's, but Hannah Cartwright became as familiar in culinary circles as Chloe Cartwright was in the literary world. We chopped and stirred and tasted, side by side. We browsed through recipes in bed, but the only official position I accepted was that of sous chef. I didn't want a marriage upgrade.

Daniel and Hannah boosted business at Gabrielle's. I can't brag that it had a prime time slot but any slot on a national station is helpful. We'd built up quite a following, judging by the emails. That was one of my contributions to the business plan. I'm a techno-wizard, compared to Daniel. I grew up in a house where a computer overshadowed all other domestic appliances in terms of usage. I knew my way around a keyboard long before I learned how to sauté vegetables or spin sugar to decorate a dessert. I answered every single email personally. Every blog. Every entry on Facebook. It was part of our formula to build our customer base. It was one of the first things to fall by the wayside as my mother began to elbow her way into my routine on a daily basis.

She'd already had her diagnosis a few years before *Daniel and Hannah* was launched, but she still seemed intermittently on the ball. That's a complicating factor with Alzheimer's. We weren't sure how worried we should be about her fluctuating symptoms.

The *Daniel and Hannah* program was the brainchild of Hugh Armstrong who was a big deal in program planning at M-Web and was, fortuitously, a regular at Gabrielle's. This particular brief was to promote tourism ahead of the World Cup which was still a distant blip on the radar at that stage. It was sponsored by the national tourist board and there were segments in each show to promote Joburg, Cape Town and Durban.

"Our aim is to create an impression of national diversity," Hugh explained with his characteristic enthusiasm, when he first broached Daniel about the show. "I've already got a perfect couple who run an Indian restaurant in Kloof and an old Chinese woman and her son who run a take-away in Parktown North."

"But Joburg's hardly Chinese!" I protested.

"We're going to portray it as city on the move. A hotch-potch of nationalities where no one ever goes to bed. A takeaway culture like New York. And these guys don't do burger and chips. They're authentic Chinese. With platters to die for. They make a fortune. It's a madhouse. Gabrielle's is going to be a complete contrast. Laidback Cape Town with traditional recipes which have been simmering since the last century..."

There are dozens of restaurants in Cape Town which would have fitted this particular branding, but color's still an issue in South Africa, however long ago apartheid is supposed to have ended. There aren't many black chefs. Especially those who trained in Paris and own a restaurant. It's a plus if the girlfriend/assistant chef is white. And the daughter of a well-known figure in literary circles. Hugh thought would be a marketable brand. He even liked our names.

My mother phoned one of her buddies on the Cape Times after the show was aired for the first time and sure enough, she pitched up to deliver a review. It takes up a whole page in my mother's scrapbook. She read it out to any of her luckless mates who dropped in for a cup of coffee.

Daniel and Hannah *are already an established feature for diners frequenting the increasingly vibey area around Long Street in Cape Town. Daniel Mbu, the new owner of Long Street's landmark bistro, Gabrielle's, is a product of Southern Sun's BEE initiative to encourage local culinary skills. Part of the Mbu magic is his accent; the son of refugees from the Congo, his home language is French. He doesn't wear a beret, but his cooking has the flair traditionally associated with France.*

I don't come over quite as well as the maestro, but it was complimentary enough to keep my mother reading out loud to anyone who would listen.

Hannah Cartwright is one of Mbu's most critical ingredients. "She has an exceptional sense of taste," says Mbu. "She knows exactly what's missing in a dish—and doesn't hesitate to tell me!" he jokes ruefully. You can understand why she's indispensable. She's everywhere - charming the guests with her trademark smile as she chats, circulates and recommends. And her recommendations shouldn't be taken lightly. She's officially employed as an assistant chef and can turn her hand to everything from flambé fillet at the table to tossing pancakes in cinnamon in a recipe gleaned from her Muslim neighbour in the Bo-Kaap where she grew up.

"Did you actually say I was your most essential ingredient?" I asked Daniel suspiciously when I read the review for the first time.

"I would have said it if I'd thought of it," said Daniel defensively.

"I said it," interrupted my mother. "She asked me to vet the article before she submitted it. I thought it was a nice touch. I am a famous author, after all. You have to use all the resources you have at your disposal."

The three of us laughed triumphantly as we poured over the review. We poured a few drinks at the same time, in honor of the occasion. We had a similar celebration with Daniel's parents at the dining room table in Khayelitsha. Karl said he and Pocahontas stuck a copy on their fridge. Everyone in my ever-extending family circle was very happy about the Hannah and Daniel connection

I was the only one who didn't want to make it official.

>

NINETEEN

It's inevitable that I've given memory a lot of thought. What's normal. What's cause for concern. I should publish a spectrum of forgetting.

Wilful forgetfulness wouldn't make it to even the lower end of the chart. Wilful forgetfulness is simply a ploy for avoiding blame. It's basically lying. Our teachers lost count of the homework assignments Karl and I forgot to hand in on time. It suited my mother's budget to forget to pay my ballet fees. She didn't forget the PTA. She just didn't want to go. Our family perfected the technique of wilful forgetfulness, long before we ever heard of Alzheimer's.

I've put butterfly moments on the scale, but at the lower end. Everyone forgets the name of their oldest friend once in a while. It's on a par with losing your car keys or forgetting what you've come to buy at Pick n Pay. I remember my mother forgetting the name of the librarian she'd worked with for a decade when she took me to the opening of a new wing in the library in Khayelitsha.

At that time, she was canvassing the corporates for donations to buy books. I was with her the day she went to unload her latest haul to that library.

"This is my daughter, Hannah," beamed my mother as the librarian bustled effusively up to look at the spoils. "And this is...this is..."

There was a pause. I knew at once that she'd been afflicted with one of those dreadful lapses when a name or word with which you are utterly familiar escapes you. Everyone has them. Butterfly moments, I call them, where the word in question hovers on gossamer wings on the edge of your consciousness, tantalizingly out of reach. I leapt into the awkward silence with praiseworthy creativity.

"There's no need for introductions here," I gushed. "Mom's talked about you so much over the years that it feels as if we're old friends!" I threw my arms around the startled librarian as my mother rolled her eyes gratefully in the background. The moment passed as the headmaster ushered us along to have a look at the room that had been designated as the library. We were halfway down the corridor when my mother suddenly paused in mid-sentence and yelled "Sylvia!" to no one in particular. She made it sound as if she'd had some universal revelation, like Einstein when he cried, "Eureka!" The butterflies had obviously made a sudden return with the missing name.

Everyone turned around and stared at her. The Sylvia

in question looked understandably confused. My mother and I were overcome with a fit of giggles. We pulled ourselves together when Sylvia opened the door to her library. The newly installed shelves looked great – but they were completely empty. Not a single book. I realized for the first time what a difference my mother's donation would make. Bedtime stories had been part of growing up with a mother like mine, but Goldilocks and Cinderella must seem less relevant to children living with their families in a single room. They know all about sex, drunkenness and violence long before they're able to read crime fiction.

I wish my mother had been able to see that the books she gave them made a difference in their lives, but her butterfly moments had started to multiply since our visit. I don't know if there's a collective noun for butterflies, but it seemed as if a multitude had gathered in my mother's head. They helped themselves to half the words in her once extensive vocabulary. It wasn't long before Sylvia wasn't the only name, and word, she couldn't remember.

➤

The problem with having grown up with a mad mother is that we'd grown accustomed to behavior which might have seemed bizarre to other people. We just shrugged our shoulders and filed another incident in the family archive. That's why we weren't anxious about the incident on the *Symphony* when Daniel and I were invited to give a presentation to the guests on the voyage between Cape Town and Durban. It seemed no worse than forgetting to shut the door to keep the dogs out of the traffic.

We'd become semi-celebrities, thanks to *Daniel and Hannah*. Daniel's a marketable brand, but the invitations had to include me because my name was in the title. We persuaded my mother to join us on the cruise. We thought she'd be able to cope with both of us around to keep an eye on her. We made our way up the gangplank to shake hands with the crew waiting to welcome us aboard. We threw streamers from the deck and sipped a glass of sparkling wine as the Symphony set sail from Cape Town harbor. The sea was an impossible shade of blue beneath the mountain, tinged in shades of pink by the dipping sun. Cruising was a new experience for all three of us.

"Where's your mother?" asked Daniel as he opened the well-stocked fridge in our lovely suite on the evening following our presentation. She was scheduled to join us in her glad rags, prior to making our way to the captain's table.

"She was having tea on Deck Four. She said she knew where the cabin was. Maybe she fell overboard on her way back?" I answered as I took the offered drink. I started to feel anxious. I shouldn't have left her but sometimes she seemed just like her old self. And our cabin was so close to the tea-room...

"She'll be here in a minute," said Daniel reassuringly as we settled ourselves on our deckchairs to admire the sun slipping below the horizon. We made desultory conversation, pretending we weren't really afraid that she had somehow leapt into the sea while our backs were turned.

Daniel looked at his watch. "Phone her. Maybe she is

overboard after all. Listen for the sound of waves in the background..."

"This is probably a futile exercise." I dialled her number. "The chances of her having her phone switched on are close to zero." But I underestimated her. She answered on the second ring.

"Where the hell are you?" she demanded when she heard my voice. "We were supposed to meet here at six."

"But we're here," I protested. "Where are you? We've been shouting, "Man overboard!" down all the corridors."

"You are not here," she protested indignantly. "And it's half-past six already."

"But we are here, Mom! We've been here for half an hour. You're the one who's missing."

"Don't be ridiculous," said my mother, beginning to snarl. "There's no one else here."

"Where are you?" I asked with a sense of foreboding.

"Where am I? I'm in the cabin of course. I'm on the balcony having a scotch. There's no one else here. Unless you're both under the bed, you're in the wrong cabin."

"We are not in the wrong cabin, Mom," I assured her. "Our clothes are lying all over the bed. What cabin are you in, for God's sake?"

"I'm in your cabin. Number...number...oh, I can't remember the fucking number. But it's definitely your cabin. I recognize the furniture."

"They're all furnished the same," I told her. "Open a cupboard! Look at the clothes! Look at the luggage! Can you see anything you recognize?"

I heard her wrench open a drawer. There was a moment's silence.

"Oh Christ!" she wailed. "These aren't your clothes! They'd fit a midget! You should see this underwear! I think I must be in the honeymoon suite!"

"Get out, for God's sake! How did you get in?"

"The maid was here!" she said. "I told her I'd forgotten my key. I had a long chat with her! She's from Eastern Europe! The poor girl will probably be fired! I've helped myself to a couple of those expensive little scotches they stock the fridge with. And some pretzels too! They'll think she stole them!"

"What's the cabin number? "I asked her.

"I don't know the fucking number," she protested. "I don't even know my own number! How do you expect me to know the number of the honeymoon suite?"

"Look on the phone!"

"Ah ha!" she cried after what seemed like an inordinate pause. She obviously couldn't find the phone. "It's 763." She wanted me come to fetch her. With money. "I must pay for the scotch and the pretzels. I'm worried about my little Romanian!" She was writing an apologetic note on the notepad when I burst into cabin 763.

Sorry about the invasion. Wrong cabin. Thanks for the scotch and pretzels. Don't blame the maid. PS Nice underwear...

"You can't put that! You sound like a pervert rifling through their drawers."

"They won't know it's me unless they DNA the entire

boat," said my mother.

We peered out of the door and looked right and left down the corridor. "All clear!" said my mother. We were giggled like errant schoolgirls on our way back to join Daniel in 736.

I don't rate the cabin incident highly on my Spectrum of Forgetting. Anyone can get lost on a ship the size of the Symphony. And my mother had a point about the cabins. The furnishings are uniform. They do all look the same at first glance.

I wrote it off as amusing anecdote.

There are other incidents which might seem minor but rank higher on my spectrum. Like the time she paused, during her endless paging through her scrapbook. She seemed transfixed by one of the photos from her university days at Sussex. It was a full page black and white photo from a student newspaper. It featured Mbeki, his arm draped around my father's shoulders. They both looked so young! My father had shoulder-length hair, was togged out in a kaftan and was smoking what was probably a noxious weed. Mbeki was wearing a tweed jacket and a cloth cap, with a pipe in the corner of his mouth.

"Who's the man with Mbeki?" my mother asked. I couldn't believe my ears. Why would her memory rank a random politician above the father of her children?

Alzheimer's is a complicated illness.

➤

TWENTY

I've started to rank my own memories according to the impact they've had on the way my life has unfolded.

I have lots of memories of Daniel asking me to marry him. I wonder now why I said no with such consistency, despite the advice I got from everyone who loved me most.

Maybe I should blame my father. My absent father, looking down his handsome nose at me from every second wall in the house. He was never real. Perhaps that's why I grew up with unrealistic expectations of what a husband should be. Someone at the same romantic distance as my father. Someone very different from Daniel.

I saw him every single day. We worked with candles and long-stemmed roses, but they were all for the customers. There wasn't much romance over the stove when a sauce curdled unexpectedly or if the meat wasn't as tender as butter. God help us all if a customer complained. I was exposed to Daniel at much closer quarters than the photos of my father on the passage wall.

I can't blame my friends for giving me what I thought was bad advice.

"Marry him!" chorused Julia and Mary when they got to know him. They were home to Cape Town on holiday. "He's so gorgeous!" they warned me. "He'll ride off into the sunset with the new waitress on the block!" My mother nodded.

I remember a long conversation about marriage that I had with my mother, shortly after she got her diagnosis. Hearing you have a terminal illness must make you think back on the life you will be leaving, sooner than anticipated. It was one of her coherent days.

"I wish you'd marry Daniel," she mused. We were at a pavement café in Long Street, sipping cappuccinos.

"Why is everyone so obsessed with marriage?" I sighed. "You haven't been married for as long as I've known you. Why didn't you marry Andrew? Or Simon? They both hung around for long enough. Why didn't you marry one of them, if marriage has so much to recommend it?"

My mother sighed. "I haven't been a very good role model, have I." It was more of a statement than a question.

"Rubbish!" I said protectively. You start to value your mother when you learn that there is a strong likelihood you are going to lose her. "You were the best mother on the block. Julia and Mary always hoped you'd adopt them."

"We both know that isn't true," she said wearily.

"Children need a fulltime mother," she added. "And I was never that. You grew up in a blur. I cried for two whole years after Anton died. I cried every time I changed your nappy. I cried because he'd never see you, with all your brand new teeth and your hallelujah smile. I was so wrapped up in my own grief that I didn't give you the attention a baby needs. Someone should have reported me to social welfare."

"Oh, Mom," I said, stricken with empathy, as much as guilt. I'd enjoyed my semi-orphan status. I don't think I'd registered the extent of her loss and grief. A miscellany of secrets tumbled out that night. "I thought you loved Karl best," I admitted. "But so did I. Everyone did. Julia and Mary only came to see me on the off-chance that he was home."

"You are talking absolute rubbish, darling." my mother protested fondly. "You were everyone's favorite. You had us all wrapped around your finger," she added, smiling. But then her face clouded. It was definitely time for shedding secrets.

"I did favor Karl," she admitted. "But not because I loved him more. It's hard to explain, even to myself. People always think it's because he looks so much like Anton, but I hate that explanation. It sounds like incest. As if Karl was some sort of replacement for Anton. That's nonsense. Loving your husband is completely different from loving your children. Any mother on the planet will tell you that you have enough love inside you to love both your children. All your children. Julia's mom and Fatima

177

had twice as many children as me and they had plenty of love to go round. But I loved Karl especially because he had to grow up without Anton."

"But so did I!" I protested.

"I know, it doesn't make sense," she admitted. "Even to me. But nothing made sense then. Anton's death didn't make any sense at all. Karl kept asking me where Daddy had gone. He wasn't even six years old. All his friends had fathers who pitched up to watch the soccer on Saturday mornings. He kept asking me where Daddy was. I promised him that I would always be there to watch. It became a sort of fetish. I used to break my neck to get to his fucking fixtures. Then he stopped asking me about Anton and that made it even worse. It made me even more determined to be there."

"But what about me?" I persisted. "You hardly ever came to ballet."

"I could make something up," said my mother, after a long pause, "but the true answer is that I didn't have time. My priorities seem inconceivable in retrospect, but you were such an easy child. You seemed perfectly happy to come along to all Karl's fixtures. Or to protest at the cathedral. To sit in a corner and color in while I did an interview. You were just a baby when Anton died so you couldn't ask where he'd gone. It suited me to think you couldn't miss your father."

"I didn't miss him." I said. Truthfully.

My mother scooped the foam from her cappuccino before she continued. "You say you didn't miss him. And that's what I thought. You and Karl were such charming children. Everyone loved you. That's what kept me going whenever I made another monumental cock-up. I thought, at least I'd done well with you and Karl."

"You did do well," I insisted. "That's why it doesn't seem necessary to get married."

"Being married is different," said my mother, sounding owl-like. "It's too easy to walk out if you're living together. If you're married, you have to fill in divorce papers or whatever you have to do to get divorced. It must be even more complicated than getting a new ID and God knows, that's bad enough. You can't just get divorced on a whim so you try harder to fix the problem. I'd like it to be impossible for you to leave Daniel. Or vice versa."

"Daniel's not the only man in the world," I protested. "I don't believe in the concept of a one and only. My father's not the only man you've ever loved, even though he's the only one you married."

"I've been thinking about that," said my mother. "Now that..." Her voice trailed off. "Now that I'm sick," she continued. We both knew she meant now that she was dying. "I wouldn't marry again because I put your father and marriage on a pedestal. The whole concept of marriage was linked to him. Like a special private altar. No one else was allowed to go there. I had to get on with my life, but not getting married became a fetish. It seems ridiculous in retrospect."

"Do you regret not marrying again?" I asked her. "I never felt sorry for you because you didn't have a husband. You had so many projects on the go. There were always people around. You were never on your own."

"I want you to know what extra dimensions being married gives you because I never gave you the chance to see for yourselves," she explained. "You and Karl missed out on first-hand exposure to marriage because you didn't grow up with married parents. Marriage is an upgrade of friendship. Like you have with Julia and Mary but with sex thrown into the package. Exclusive sex," she added pointedly. No doubt every mother has reservations about a daughter who's been sleeping around since her teenage seduction by her best friend's pimpled brother.

She sighed before picking up the thread. "Perhaps that's one of the worst mistakes I made as a mother. Neither you nor Karl have any concept of fidelity, living with me. But you don't have to make the same mistake as me. I don't hold out much hope for Karl and Pocahontas, but I'd like to believe that you and Daniel are in it for the long term."

I wish I'd married Daniel, if only to have given her that assurance. But I didn't want to. I couldn't see that marriage would make any difference to what we had already. I couldn't face a wedding. Daniel's family is so Catholic that I was afraid they'd hire a cathedral. They'd tog me out in white satin and Mary and Julia would fly over from London to be bridesmaids.

And as time slipped by, my mother became a risky proposition at a wedding. I knew Daniel's mother would buy her a pink hat and install her in the front pew. I was afraid she might interrupt the service and accuse the priest of stealing the ring.

I wouldn't marry Daniel, no matter how often he asked me. I could have made my mother happy, but it's too late now. I was too stupid to recognize a knight in shining armor because he was disguised as my best friend.

>

TWENTY-ONE

I've never had to watch someone die of cancer. But, as I lay under the duvet, trying to fall asleep after a bad day with my mother, I thought it would be better if she had cancer. At least the doctor could put up a drip or administer chemotherapy. At least I would feel that some measures were being taken. Even if all her hair fell out.

But there was nothing I could do to help my mother. I felt guilty because she drove me mad. I hated being with her. She followed me around and repeated everything I said. She kept asking me what the time was. It drove me insane.

There wasn't a wizard anywhere who could wave a magic wand and change her into different person. Alzheimer's is more sinister than that. Insidious, like a dripping tap. But even the sandstone on Table Mountain wears away eventually. By the time the changes have happened, it's too late to turn around and head back in the opposite direction.

I couldn't find her when I got to Pepper Street that day. I was later than I'd planned to be. I'd told Dorothy she could take a break, but I'd been delayed at Gabrielle's. Matters were getting out of hand as I tried to keep an eye on my mad mother at the same time as running a business. It was imperative for me to check the supplies in the fridge. And in the cupboards. To check on the staff. To do their salaries. Being in two places at one time seemed to have become integral to my job description by then. Thank God my boss was Catholic. Daniel always forgave me when he found yet another ingredient missing for his signature dishes, but everyone could see his patience was starting to wear thin.

"Mom?" I called with growing anxiety. I knew Dorothy could be relied on to lock all the doors when she left, but it wasn't inconceivable that my mother had somehow contrived to squeeze through a window. I couldn't suppress a feeling of outrage when I found her in a corner of my bedroom which had remained untouched since I moved in with Daniel. I know she can't help it, but it still seemed like an invasion when I saw that she'd opened my secret drawer. The contents were spilled in confusion on the carpet where she was sitting.

"What are you doing, Mom?" I asked tightly, trying not to raise my voice. She had become increasingly sensitive to any change in tone. I was angry, but I didn't want to make her cry. I always lock my drawer, but its tiny silver key is clearly visible in a china bowl on top of the dresser.

I didn't bother to hide it. Who was going to unlock it, after all?

My mother, apparently.

She'd wrenched the drawer right out of the dresser so the contents were scattered around her. The music box. The ballet shoes. The scarlet g-string, along with a miscellany of sexy underwear. Tiny bikinis, like you'd see on Clifton. Slinky tops and a little red dress. My mother had opened the music box. Her face was creased in a smile as she watched the ballerina revolve to gentle music.

I snapped the box shut. The music stopped abruptly. My mother's eyes registered the sudden silence. They came into focus. Brief flashes of absolute lucidity were one of the most disconcerting aspects of her illness as it developed. But her words were a contradiction.

"You were such a wonderful dancer, my darling," she told me, her voice permeated with a fondness that wrung my heart and made me regret my anger. Her long fingers picked up one of Julia's stolen shoes. "Look how small your feet were! I remember your tiny dainty feet!"

I took the shoe out of hand. "You don't remember my tiny dainty feet," I told her firmly. "I'm Hannah. I never had tiny, dainty feet. You're getting me mixed up with Julia. These are her shoes. Not mine."

But my mother continued as if I hadn't spoken. "Encore!" she shouted, raising her voice to a higher pitch than before. "Encore! Our little fairy! Encore, we shouted! Everyone clapped! Encore! Encore!" she repeated, still with the beatific smile.

I stared at her. She'd triggered a memory. A long discarded memory of my solitary performance in a tutu, shortly after Julia and I had started lessons. My solo had been no more individual than a squad of lemmings hurling themselves over a cliff. Our ballet teacher had a strategy designed to persuade the parents that the money they forked out for lessons was paying dividends. Each member of the class was choreographed to step out from the chorus line for a brief pirouette or two on her own. There were flashlights going off all night at the Christmas concert.

There'd been the sort of crisis you'd expect in our house over my costume which was tacked together at the last possible moment.

"Fucking fairies," moaned my mother as we feverishly glued tinsel into place on my gossamer wings. Karl is five years older than me so he was already over six feet tall at the start of my brief career as a ballet soloist. He looked ridiculous, hunched over my mother's ancient Elna, trying to machine the seams on my pink net tutu.

I remember counting out the routine with grim determination until it was my turn to take center stage. I lifted my arms above my head and did my scheduled twirling. My mother and Karl stood up and shouted "Encore!" I felt as if I were at a command performance for the queen! I remember the laughter. Widespread clapping. A wild hissing from the wings as I sank into a second curtsey.

"Hannah! Get back in line!"

My heart twisted in a knot. I was touched that so

trivial an incident was lodged in a mind as muddled as my mother's. And then she surprised me even more. She continued running her fingers through the silky contents of the drawer.

"So soft," she murmured. "Why has everything still got a price tag?" she asked.

I stared at her in amazement. How could she have focused on such a tiny detail when she struggled to remember where we kept the tea bags in the kitchen?

It seemed as if I was on yet another trip to Wonderland with Alice so I told her the truth. Perhaps living with a Catholic had triggered an instinct to confess. Or, more probably, I knew that it didn't matter what I told her. A batwing would shift across her mind and lucidity would vanish. She would never remember this conversation.

"I stole them," I said. "I never took the price tags off because I never wore any of them. They were all too small for me."

"How pointless," said my mother, with uncharacteristic practicality. "Why didn't you steal a bigger size?" Her morality was still suspect, even now her mind was going. She didn't seem at all perturbed to hear that her daughter was a serial thief.

"I wanted them to fit me," I explained. "They would have fit Julia. Or Mary. I wanted to be the same size as them."

"How ironic," said my mother coherently. As if she were still a famous author with all her facilities intact. "Julia was desperate to be like you. She cried on my lap because she was so flat-chested. I told her that her boobs would grow, but they never did. Poor little Julia. Poor Mary. You overshadowed both of them."

I stared at her disbelievingly. The madness was definitely back. "I was the size of a block of flats," I reminded her. "With a hawk nose. I felt like an overweight parrot whenever I saw myself in the mirror."

"You and Karl have your father's nose," she remarked. I couldn't disagree, but I pointed out that it looked better on a boy than on a girl.

"Nonsense!" said my mother briskly "True beauty needs an outstanding feature. Look at the size of Julia Robert's mouth." This was definitely the first time I'd been compared to Julia Roberts. The delusions kept coming. "You were never fat," she asserted. "Voluptuous, but never fat. Remember how Karl's friends used to follow you around."

I didn't bother to tell her that this was because I was such an easy lay. I'd stopped confessing by then. I sensed that lucidity was over for my mother for the day. Her eyes clouded. Her mind shifted. Changed down a gear.

"Stolen goods," she whispered as she continued to finger my spoils. "They stole the vote you know," she confided, as if I were a fellow conspirator. "They stole the colored vote..." Her voice trailed off into silence.

The shutters had dropped. My mother was back on her solitary planet.

➤

TWENTY-TWO

Incidents rank high on my spectre of forgetting because of their consequences. My mother's illness started to have a ripple effect on both my relationship with Daniel and my career. Our mutual career.

Chefs should come packaged with a warning label tattooed on their foreheads: "BEWARE OF MIDNIGHT SCHEDULE!" This should be printed in block capitals, especially if the chef in question owns the restaurant he works in. He can't go home once he's drizzled chocolate over the last order of the day. He has to hang around to lock up after stragglers. He can't maintain a girlfriend who turns into a pumpkin when the clock strikes midnight.

That's what I'd say if anyone asked me to explain the longevity of my affair with Daniel. Both of us trifled with other relationships along the way, but it was a challenge for either of us to keep pace with a lover who worked from nine to five. Daniel was the one I moaned to during my fling with James – an accountant with a serious cycling hobby. He wanted me to get out of bed at five in the morning to cycle over Chapman's peak and glory in the sunrise. I'd rather be consumed in the flames of hell. James didn't last long and neither did Numisa. She was a contestant on the *Face of Africa* so I could understand why Daniel fancied her. But they had no future.

"What she really wants is an escort," Daniel complained as we whipped egg white and folded in the cream. "She wants to be seen at every gala function on the calendar, and they all coincide with the hours I work."

I wasn't sorry to see the last of Numisa. Daniel missed her for a while, but we found it was easier for the two of us to come home together after locking up at Gabrielle's. We got into the habit of sharing our beds only with the dogs. The recipe worked well until I started adding increasingly large doses of my mother into the mix.

➤

There were problems even before I was forced to leave Daniel, to move home to look after my mother on a fulltime basis. Hiring Dorothy had seemed like finding the treasure in Aladdin's cave, but my mother became increasingly difficult to manage as her dementia flexed its fingers and tightened its clutch.

"You must come home, Hannah," became Dorothy's standard opening line. I began to flinch whenever her name came up on my cell phone. This happened with increasing frequency at the start of my evening shift.

Sundowning takes on a whole new meaning when you're caring for a patient with Alzheimer's. It's classic symptom, once the illness become firmly established. Patients become increasingly disorientated when the afternoon merges with the evening. I won't forget the night M-Net decided to screen *Daniel and Hannah* live from Gabrielle's.

I'd made a hair appointment. I always had my hair done before they filmed an episode. No one wants to be beamed out on national television with greasy hair. The phone rang as I was making my way to the car. I looked particularly dreadful. I always put off washing my hair when I'm seeing the hairdresser later. I'd skulked around, undercover, secure in the knowledge that transformation was on the horizon. I'd timed everything so that I'd be back home to change, well before the scheduled start. That was before the phone rang.

"I think you better come," said Dorothy without preamble.

"I can't come now," I said despairingly. "What's the matter? I'm just on my way to the hairdresser. I can't come now."

"You must come," said Dorothy firmly. And then she put the phone down.

"Christ," I muttered to myself as I reversed down the drive. "I can't handle this today."

I'm lucky I wasn't arrested for speeding as I screeched to a halt on Pepper Street in record time. Perhaps I wasn't so lucky. Maybe jail would have been a soft option under the circumstances. Dorothy's nose was bleeding when she opened the door.

"She didn't mean to hit me," she said at once. She was very protective of her mad patient. Everyone had always loved my mother, but she grew less lovable every time I saw her. It's hard to get used to a different version of the person you've known all your life.

"She's mixed up," said Dorothy, dabbing ineffectually at her bleeding nose." She can't remember where she is. She can't remember who I am. She thinks I'm locking her up. She was trying to get outside, and I had to lock the door to stop her going into the street. She was struggling with me and her arm hit my face. She didn't mean to hit me," she insisted.

"But where is she now?" I asked, dabbing equally ineffectually at the blood. Dorothy gestured helplessly at the closed door to the bedroom.

"I had to lock her in," she said.

My heart twisted when I opened the door. My mother was curled in a fetal position on the edge of the large double bed. She lashed out at me when I touched her, but she calmed down when she recognized my face. I stroked her gently. I felt her coiled back, the tension in her shoulders.

I sat and stroked some more, but I also kept looking at my watch. I was already half an hour late for my hair appointment. I held my breath as her eyes closed. I carried on stroking until I dared to hope that she was asleep. Her eyes snapped open the minute I tried to slink out of the room. Her wail was thin. Heartbreak material. She stopped immediately when I resumed stroking.

And so it went on, as I tried desperately to extricate myself. Stop and start. It was blackmail. I called Dorothy.

"I'm afraid I really have to go," I told her.

"But she's all right when you're here," Dorothy pointed out, her nose still streaked with blood.

I stroked a bit more. Looked at my watch. My hair appointment had gone out of the window but what about my clothes? I couldn't face the cameras in my baggy tracksuit.

"I have to go," I said. I tried to ignore the reproach in Dorothy's eyes as I walked past her. I tried to ignore my mother's wailing which increased in volume as I made my way to the car. I flinched as I looked back at the house. My mother was standing at the bedroom window, hands pressed beseechingly against the glass. Like a prisoner. I could see Dorothy behind her, trying to pry her away.

My cell was ringing. Daniel's name came up on the screen as I snatched it up.

"Where are you?" he snarled. "They're already setting up. Where the hell are you?"

"My mother," I whispered. "I can't leave my mother."

"What?" he said, incredulously. "You have to leave her. This is a live broadcast. You have to leave her! Where's Dorothy?"

I started the engine. I didn't look to see if my mother was still trying to get out of the window. The tears were hot against my cheeks as I made my way to Gabrielle's. I'm sure the camera crew winced as I made my late, dishevelled entry, minutes before the show was due to air.

Daniel definitely winced. He looked immaculate in black and white. I had an equally immaculate outfit, freshly ironed on its hanger in our bedroom but it was too late to worry about that now.

I was hustled into position. I snatched up a knife and started chopping onions. I wished I was dicing myself into tiny pieces.

Or my mother.

The compere swung into his patter, welcoming viewers to this edition of *Daniel and Hannah*, live from Gabrielle's in Cape Town. I noticed that the cameras didn't dwell too long on the Hannah aspect. The attention was all on Daniel who was fortuitously as suave and articulate as usual. Only I knew he was ruffled underneath his smile. I continued to decimate the onions while he waxed on about the dish we'd decided to present.

"Tonight, we're introducing you to the wonders of capers," he began. "I discovered fresh capers while exploring Cyprus. It's as barren as any other Greek island. So I couldn't help noticing the lush bushes which were somehow thriving in the cracks of the rock face. The leaves are grey and waxy, but there were buds on the leaves and some had opened up into the most delicate pink flowers. The flowers were nothing short of spectacular. They cascaded over the bare rock face. Those buds are what we pickle and salt to bottle capers as we know them. I always have some bottles of Pantelleria capers in my pantry. They are key to the special flavor of the dish we're making tonight – a tomato and brinjal bake. It's a mouth-watering dish served fresh from the oven, but the flavors develop even more overnight, if any of you busy housewives want to whip this up the day before the dinner party."

"We'll start with aubergines," he continued with authority, taking off the cover of the wicker basket where we stored the vegetables.

He paused. And then he looked at me.

"Hannah?" he said with a question in his voice. "Where did you put the aubergines?" The camera followed the direction of his voice. Honed in on me. On my greasy hair. M baggy tracksuit.

"Oh Christ!" I said distinctly as the cameras beamed me out on national television. During family hour. "I forgot the fucking aubergines..."

The cameras swivelled away. Somehow, no one managed to faint outright. God knows what happened next because I left. They're lucky I didn't damage family hour even more by plunging the chopping knife into my heart. Or the camera-man's...

I slammed the knife down beside the onions and stormed out of the restaurant. I wept my way down to our favorite café. I was still drooping at our table when Daniel tracked me down after the shoot ended. I'd had seven cups of coffee by then and was starting my second carafe of wine. He paid my bill and took me home.

Daniel was my gold mine. And it had nothing to do with the salary he paid me.

The story made the Sunday paper. *"Hannah in hot water!"* It wasn't on the front page, but it was bad enough.

It quoted me swearing with all the @#$% symbols they use to block out the four letter words that celebrities inadvertently use in public places. But it wasn't as much of a disaster for Gabrielle's as I imagined it would be. Still, I slunk around apologizing abjectly to Daniel or anyone else within earshot.

I could have tried to cast blame on my mother for my delinquency, but it was actually thanks to her that M-Net didn't can the show. My mother's semi-famous in the literary world. Some anonymous person on the staff told a reporter that I was under a lot of strain because she had Alzheimer's. The newspapers liked that bit of gossip. It was enough to shut up any critic. Everyone felt sorry for me. The incident evolved into a standing joke with some of the regular customers. "Any fucking aubergines on the menu tonight, Hannah?" they'd tease as I took their orders.

It would all have blown over if it had been the only time it happened.

➤

TWENTY-THREE

Dorothy dissolved in tears when my mother accused her of stealing T-shirts and listening in to her conversations on the phone. I couldn't expect her to stay. It wasn't her mother after all. Mom was all mine. I said goodbye to Daniel and his darling dogs and moved back home to watch the disintegration of my mother at closer quarters.

Daniel warned that I was taking on more than I could handle.

"I know you love her, Hannah," he told me as I lay in a despondent heap on the couch after she'd eventually wandered off to bed. I didn't have the energy to contemplate a multiple orgasm as a way to lift my spirits. "I love her too. But what about us? When am I going to see you? The dogs have gone into a decline. I'm going to have to get them antidepressants from the vet. They miss you. I miss you too."

I went into a decline myself at the mere mention of

the dogs. I needed some pet therapy almost as much as I needed Daniel. I became unpleasantly aggressive.

"And what do you suggest I do?" I demanded. "Shall I buy a gun and shoot her?" I was at the end of my tether. There were days when I wished I'd wake up to find she'd disappeared.

"There are professionals who are qualified to take care of her," he reminded me gently.

"You mean put her in a home?" I said angrily. I dreamed of putting her in a home virtually every waking moment of the day, but I was too ashamed to admit it to Daniel.

"Hannah," he continued. "Chloe isn't really old. I know the doctor said patients with this form of Alzheimer's can die earlier, but physically, she's fine. She could live for another ten years. You can't seriously consider opting out of your own life for another ten years. You're exhausted after only ten days. Even three years is too long."

I knew he was right, but I was stubborn. Putting her in a home seemed like brushing her under the carpet. I refused to listen to him or Karl. They could both see that my mother and I were falling off a cliff. There were days when I was tempted to push her over, but she'd stopped suggesting that by the time it became a really seductive option.

>

It's hard not to feel jealous of other people, even if they're your best friends.

I hadn't felt jealous of Mary when she phoned from

London to tell me she was pregnant. Incredulity was the only emotion I'd registered. I was gobsmacked. Even as a teenager, Mattress Mary would have qualified to write a bible on how to avoid pregnancy. How could my streetwise friend possibly have fallen pregnant in a world jam-packed with contraceptives devices?

But Mary merely shrugged her trans-Atlantic shoulders before double gob-smacking my disbelieving ears. She had no abortion plans.

"But you HATE babies!" I'd protested when she told me she was going ahead with the pregnancy. "And what about your job? Are actuaries actually allowed to be actuaries if they have a baby under the desk?" I've never grasped what an actuary does. All I knew was that they paid her a fortune to do it.

"Hasn't working remotely reached South Africa yet?" she responded, sounding exasperated. But I don't think she was as cool about her new persona as she sounded. She sounded a lot less cool when I asked how Simon felt about her decision. Simon had been Mary's on/off boyfriend for a couple of years by then. She admitted that Richard had been a feature during a recent off-period which involved a weekend excursion to some actuarial conference in Paris.

"I'm not altogether sure it's Simon's," she confided. Before bursting into tears. Bursting into tears has never been one of Mary's trademark features.

"Surely that makes abortion even more the obvious choice?" I queried. I was, as I may have mentioned, utterly gobsmacked by this turn of events.

More tears.

"It's made me think," she admitted. "Rethink. I look at Julia with her starry eyes and a diamond on her finger. She's getting married. She's going to say till death do us part. And she's going to mean it. I can't imagine saying that to Simon. To anyone. Other than the CEO of a listed company on the FTSE. I've been immersed in provident funds since I was seventeen. That's almost a decade! I sometimes feel as if I'm drowning. Maybe a baby's what I need to pull me to the surface..."

"Christ, Mary!" I protested. "That's quite a gamble. Especially if you happen to be the baby. You've always said you hate babies!"

"I may have said that," she admitted, "but I don't really know what I'm talking about. I don't know any babies. I don't think I've ever met a baby. Besides, I can do anything if I set my mind to it..." I could hear the tears lurking behind her words as she recited the defence she had spun to herself in the hours when she couldn't fall asleep.

"Your mom infected me with a reading habit when I was at high school. I must have read a thousand books involving mothers who're bowled over by their babies. The moment when the pain is over. When they hand over the baby and it's YOURS! That's what I want to feel! I WILL feel that! I somehow KNOW that's how I'll feel! And I want to do it by myself..."

To say I was horrified would be an understatement. I was afraid she would unfriend me if I protested too emphatically, so I bleated out some ineffectual warnings before hanging up. I phoned Jules immediately and told her to intervene. To wield the scalpel herself if necessary. We wrung our collective hands for hours. We knew that Mattress Mary wasn't single-mother material but intervention was difficult because she was so fucking rich by then. Whenever it looked as if things were getting on top of her – a demanding job, coupled with the pressures of pregnancy – she merely opened the Yellow Pages and hired someone to help her.

Mary never had to struggle to fit in a visit to the supermarket or find time to cook a meal. It did indeed prove feasible to balance the books – or whatever actuaries have to balance – from home. It's not as if they're engineers who might need to climb up the scaffolding on a construction site. I don't have much insight into what any real job demands.

I'd been a waitress for most of my life.

Mary appeared to sail through her subsequent pregnancy and delivered a healthy son with the assistance of Julia – an obvious choice for a birth partner – when the delivery date arrived, predictably right on schedule. But, as I feared from the outset, everything became more complicated when there was a real baby, not falling asleep in the IKEA cot in the color-coordinated nursery with its mobiles and hand-painted murals. I wasn't at all surprised to hear she was coming back to Cape Town to stay with her mother for a couple of months. I wasn't convinced her high-flying mother would be much help, but it was worth a try.

I was certain my own mother wouldn't be any help at all.

Mary's new baby had evolved into a toddler by the time she arrived, but I knew how much she was looking forward to showing him off to my mother. It was a wasted exercise. My mother didn't show the slightest interest in the baby. Or even in Mary. I'm not sure she knew who Mary was.

He was still wearing a nappy. I watched as Mary changed him on the table in my mother's bedroom. She smiled down at her little boy as she lifted his chubby legs and wiped his bottom. I've never had a baby, but I love their plump bottoms and their dimples. I was impressed to see how deftly Mary handled the whole procedure. She seemed as adept in her new role as a single mom as she was as an actuary.

Nappies had remained part of my routine, even after my mother's arm came out of plaster. Some people make a career out of geriatric nursing, but I am not one of them. I was totally incompetent. I couldn't bear my new job description.

Changing her nappies was an ordeal. She'd lost a lot of weight, but she's still a big woman. I found it physically hard to lift her. And she was as difficult about having her nappy changed as she'd been about everything else in her life. She didn't suddenly become docile when she became incontinent. She'd twist and turn and make the proceedings worse than they already were. It's an invasion of privacy to change an adult's nappy – especially if she's your mother. A reversal of the natural order. Out of kilter.

I used to gag when her nappy was dirty.

I knew Mary's little boy would be different the next time I saw him. He wouldn't be wearing a nappy. He'd be walking, rather than toddling. Talking. Sweeter than ever. He'd have learned new skills. New independence. New words.

My mother would be different too. Increasingly dependent, with fewer and fewer words at her disposal. She sank deeper below luck level every day.

And I was sinking with her...

➤

The drinks evening was Daniel's idea. He said both my mother and I were in need of a diversion. "I'll ask some people round," he said in his most persuasive manner. "They all adore Chloe. They know our situation. I'll bring some snacks and you can focus on gin and conversation."

I must say it sounded tempting. I washed my hair and put on some make-up. I washed my mother's hair too and put some makeup on her face as well. I shoved the debris out of sight in the lounge while Daniel answered the doorbell. My mother tried to put her best foot forward when our friends arrived, laden with wine and good intentions.

"And what do you do for a living?" she asked Brian brightly. She'd known Brian for about a decade. He was a photographer she'd worked with on some of her magazine articles. We all pretended it was a perfectly kosher question for her to have asked.

"I'm a photographer," he told her.

"Oh yes," said my mother, as brightly as before. She'd obviously decided that brightly was going to be the tone for the evening. "Tell me about it!"

Brian launched into a brave account of his studio and his equipment.

"Oh yes," said my mother as he paused for breath. Because she continued to look expectant, he soldiered on with further photographic details. A silence fell as he ran out of details.

And then my mother asked him what he did for a living...

Everyone breathed a sigh of relief when she said she was tired, and I led her off to bed. I went straight into the kitchen to pour myself a glass of wine. I was tossing a few herbs onto one of the snack platters when Daniel sidled into the kitchen. I could see he didn't know whether to laugh or hide under the stove. The drinks evening had been his idea after all.

"Oh God," I said. "What's happened now?"

"She's back," he admitted.

"And?" I demanded.

"And there's a problem with her nightie," he admitted.

"Oh Christ," I said. "I suppose it's upside down or inside out. What does it matter, for God's sake. Just ignore it."

"She's not wearing a nightie," said Daniel baldly. "I tried to take her back to bed but she's got this fixation with Brian. She refuses to get off the couch. She wants to know what he does for a living..."

I was swamped with despair as I heard what he was saying. I felt like a drowning man when I got back into the lounge. My mother was perched on the couch next to the luckless Brian who was trying to look nonchalant and say something else about cameras while avoiding confrontation with my mother's breasts. Daniel should have been warned when he saw my mother almost in the raw that night. Large breasts don't age well. There's nothing perky about them after six decades. Old women expose their sagging breasts on beaches all over Europe, but my mother's looked totally out of place in our lounge that evening.

They had been a haven of comfort for me throughout my life. I couldn't bear to have them so cruelly exposed. My face was streaked with tears as I draped her with the cloth from the side table and led her back to bed. I got into bed with her and held her close. She kept repeating random words related to photography until she fell asleep. All the guests had gone except for Daniel by the time I went back to the lounge.

Daniel smoothed my hair and wiped my face. "Everyone understands, my darling," he assured me. But it wasn't enough that everyone understood. I couldn't bear the thought that she'd made a spectacle of herself. I knew how much she would hate it.

She was used to being in the limelight – but never as a clown.

TWENTY-FOUR

After Dorothy went back to the Transkei, we hired a day nurse to be with my mother while I was at Gabrielle's. Several day nurses. They all resigned after a couple of days. My mother screamed like a banshee whenever one arrived. The one who lasted longest could have been a stand-in for Hitler. She even looked a bit like Hitler. Minus the moustache. Unlike Dorothy, she brooked no nonsense with her patient. I was always wracked with guilt by the time I left the house, my mother's wailing echoing in my ears. I was terrified Hitler might beat my mother up when my back was turned, but I had to go to work. There was always a list of tasks I had to carry out at Gabrielle's so I tried to block my ears and drive away.

A seventieth birthday proved to be the tipping point. It all started with an innocuous phone call which I answered myself.

"Ten of you on the 19th of June? That will be fine," I

said, running my eye down our list of reservations. "And the name is?" I knocked the reservations book off the table as I scrummaged around for a pen which still worked. I scribbled "Du Plessis" on a scrap of paper as an interim measure while I gushed on in my usual manner. "May I ask if this is a special occasion, Mr. Du Plessis? Her seventieth! That's a big day! I'll make sure we have something special lined up for her!" Gush, gush, gush. Everything was very jovial as I put the phone down and bent to pick up the reservations book.

That's when my cell rang.

"You must come home, Hannah," barked Hitler. I knew better than to argue.

"Oh God!" I sighed. "What now?" Then I started paying attention. My mother had fallen. I scrabbled in my bag for my keys and rushed out, passing orders to the waitresses. I never gave Mr. Du Plessis and his family another thought.

They joined ranks with the aubergines.

I panicked all the way home. It sounded like a concussion. My mother was in enough trouble already, without adding a concussion to the mix. She was sitting on the couch when I rushed into the lounge.

"Mom!" I cried tenderly, sinking onto the seat beside her. "Are you all right?" I was horrified to see the tears on her face. But she said my name at once. It felt as if we'd won another lucky ticket on the lotto. It couldn't be a concussion if she could still remember who I was.

"It's sore," she said weakly.

"What's sore, Mom?" I asked anxiously. "Where does it hurt?" I held her hand while Hitler explained what had happened. My mom was increasingly unsteady on her feet. She'd started to look much older than she was, because she didn't wear any make-up. There was a riot when we tried to brush her hair. She seemed increasingly hostile. She didn't like anyone to touch her. She had put out her hand to stop her fall when she slipped on the tiled floor in the kitchen and banged her head on the edge of the cupboard. She seemed stunned when Hitler tried to talk to her, help her to her feet.

It seemed to be her hand that was causing pain. I phoned the ever-trusty Dr. Dave and he told me he'd meet me at the X-ray department at City Park. Her wrist was broken. They set it in plaster, and we came home.

That's when the trouble started. It was her right hand and she couldn't pull down the zip on her trousers when she went to the toilet. She couldn't pull down her pants either. Even Hitler couldn't handle the situation. My mother behaved as if she was under siege by the entire German army whenever anyone tried to help. Anyone but me. I was the only one she wanted. And pulling down my mother's pants wasn't high on the list of ways I liked to spend my time. Wiping her bottom was even lower.

➤

I didn't like to leave my mother alone while her arm was healing. She was frail and even more paranoid about everyone except me. It was Saturday night when the phone rang at Pepper Street. I recognized the voice of one of the waitresses at Gabrielle's.

"Hi, Jill," I said. "Why are you whispering?"

"I don't want Daniel to hear," she answered. I could hardly hear. She asked me if I knew anything about a table for ten. Mr. Du Plessis? I started shaking my head. Then I felt cold.

"Oh my God," I said. "I didn't write it in the book! It was the day my mom fell. I didn't write it in the book!"

Jill said it was a fiasco. The restaurant was packed to capacity, as it always was on Saturday nights. People booked weeks in advance, since the show had taken off on M-Net – despite the aubergines. Jill had the misfortune of having to tell Mr. Du Plessis that he didn't have a booking. He took the news very badly. He began to rant and rave. Every head in the restaurant was turned. It sounded as if at least ten terrorists were holding the cashier to ransom. Daniel abandoned whatever dish he was preparing in the kitchen and rushed out to solve the problem.

But it couldn't be solved. There was no room for an extra mouse in the restaurant, let alone ten angry customers.

"It's my mother's seventieth birthday!" yelled Mr. Du Plessis in righteous indignation. My brothers have come from England for the occasion! I made the booking myself! Well in advance!" And so on. And so on.

Jill said Daniel was grovelling on his knees in apology. He offered a free meal the next night. Mr. Du Plessis became incandescent with rage. You had to see his point. It would no longer be her birthday the next night. Daniel offered to find him a booking elsewhere, feverishly phoning his multiple connections. He made a reservation at a nearby restaurant and the Du Plessis entourage stormed off into the night with stiff back and promises to go public over the bad service they'd received.

"Daniel was furious," confided Jill. "You know how angry he gets," she whispered ruefully. "And I've never seen him as bad as this before. The kitchen was absolutely silent when he came back to work on the orders. We're all still creeping around like mice."

I was terrified when I put the phone down. Gabrielle's has a well-deserved reputation for excellent service. Daniel was a superb manager. He followed up personally on the merest whiff of complaint. I thought there was good chance I'd never get as old as Mr. Du Plessis' mother. I'd have a bullet through my skull by morning.

But Daniel wasn't armed when he arrived at Pepper Street well after midnight. He might not have been carrying a machine gun, but he was resolute.

"You have to put your mother into care," he told me.

I knew he was right.

TWENTY-FIVE

I was also starting to forget things. I'm now muddled about the order in which the various disasters occurred. What year did Mary come to Cape Town? How old is her little boy now? Did the Du Plessis fiasco occur before or after her visit? When did Dorothy go back to the Transkei? Am I getting Alzheimer's myself? One endless day seemed to merge with the day after. Or the day before.

I have measured out my life in coffee spoons. That's another line from some random school anthology. God knows who wrote it. Or even what it means. But I felt as if it was written with me in mind after my mother became incontinent. I scoured the Internet to find where I could buy nappies for adults in Cape Town. I unearthed Cylex with its designer range of geriatric nappies. Most people have never heard of the Cylex brand name, but it's as familiar to me now as Coca-Cola. I started pilgrimages to a Plumstead shop which sells them by the bale.

I started to measure out my life in Cylex, from one nappy change to the next. I felt very sorry for myself when my mother broke her wrist. Whenever that was. I'm too muddled to remember dates, but it tied in with Mr. Du Plessis' celebrations for his mother's birthday. Du Plessis is as poisonous a word as Cylex in my vocabulary.

I phoned Karl when I decided to put her in a home.

"It's definitely the right decision," Karl assured me. "The best thing for both of you in the long-term. It's just not feasible for you to look after her on a full-time basis. My God, I was relieved to get on a plane last March, and that was only two weeks. I don't know how you do it. You mustn't feel guilty about it. We have to face it. She's not Mom anymore."

Things must look clearer when you're living in a commune with a view of the Rockies. It didn't seem so simple from my perspective. She still had my mother's face. She smiled at me directly sometimes. She sometimes knew my name. She seemed to know that I was her daughter. Her familiar voice asked the incessant questions which drove me up the wall.

I made an appointment and drove out to Century City to have a look at a state of-the-art care center which specialized in Alzheimer's patients. I was already feeling guilty when I set out from home. My mother hated Century City. She hated the brash new buildings. "It's got no soul," she'd told me. "It's not part of Cape Town." I could almost hear her saying it as I sat in the traffic jam at the Koeberg interchange. It's a terrible interchange at any time of the day, so I had what felt like hours to consider what I was about to do.

The Oasis Care Center is like a luxury hotel. There is nowhere in the country where she would receive more professional care, but I felt like a traitor to even let it cross my mind. The manager who showed me round the center admitted that the inmates didn't fit the demographic profile of the country.

"It's not merely an economic issue," she told me. "It's cultural. Black people don't put their parents into homes when they get old because an extended family is part of their tradition." I felt guilty that it wasn't part of mine.

I must admit that the Oasis Care Center is fantastic. Everyone I spoke to was warm and kind and sympathetic about my predicament. It wasn't full. With the economic crisis, only a handful of people could afford it, even if it is part of their tradition to put their parents in a home. I was shown some immaculate bedrooms. Bright, airy and cheerful. En-suite bathrooms with a nurse on call, should an old foot stumble in the shower. There was a small intimate lounge with a high definition, flat screen TV. There were only three women sitting there at the time. They looked a lot better cared for than my mother. There was no porridge spilled on their pajamas. They weren't wearing pajamas. They were well dressed, their hair freshly cut and styled. A manicurist was painting the nails of one.

But they were completely motionless in their wheelchairs. No one was watching the television, regardless of the high-definition picture. None of them had shown even the slightest flicker of interest as we walked into the room. Their well-tended faces were closed and expressionless.

Unfocused. Intrinsically old. They were stranded on the same planet as my mother, despite the luxury of their surroundings.

It was even worse when we stepped into the immaculate lift and went down to the high-care wing. It's a hospital. A very upmarket hospital, exclusively for Alzheimer's patients. At the Oasis Care Center, old people with problems other than Alzheimer's are cared for separately. There's higher security in the Alzheimer's wing. No one could wander off to do some window shopping at Century City next door. Every ward was private. Each name was printed personally on the door. It seemed to me that their names were all they had left because all their beds had bars.

The bars freaked me out completely. As did the shouting of one of the patients. There was a nurse at her bedside trying to comfort her, but her shouting sounded desperate. Like a call for help. An incoherent call. I couldn't make any sense of the words she was shouting out. I had to turn away. It reminded me of leaving my mother at home with Hitler.

I couldn't buy a meaningful future for my mother, even if I'd managed to steal the winning Lotto ticket. If I installed her in the luxury of the Oasis Care Center, she'd have to spend the rest of her life with every face she saw a stranger. What if she didn't register that I was visiting her? What if she thought she'd been abandoned? What if she was terrified? How could I leave her lying motionless in a bed, incontinent and incoherent?

Memories of my mother swarmed like bees. My delinquent, careless mother. My talented mother with her trademark empathy and lyrical expression. I remembered the reviews, printed on the covers of the books I hadn't read. The thousand times we'd shrieked with laughter. Ten thousand cock-ups, here, there and anywhere. The people who'd streamed through Pepper Street in pursuit of one cause or another, to cry on my mother's ample shoulder. I thought of all times I'd cried there myself, in rotation on her lap with Karl and Julia and Mary. She made us feel that the world hadn't ended after all. I owed a lot to my mother.

I owed her a better death than the one that Alzheimer's had in store.

TWENTY-SIX

It's not easy to kill someone you love.

I don't think it's easy to kill anyone, even if you don't love them. Especially if you don't want to go to jail. I'd got away with stealing for years, but I wasn't sure that I could get away with murder. I believed that death would be her choice, but I'd have to live with myself. How could I do that if I killed her? Another opening line filtered through as I drove home from the Alzheimer's care center. *There are many cumbersome ways to kill a man.* It would haunt me as I tried to find a way to end my mother's life.

I can't remember when or where I saw the article, but I'd obviously filed it in my mind alongside my catalog of opening lines. It might have been online or a small feature in one of the newspapers. It wasn't headline news, but I read everything I saw about Alzheimer's. Just in case they'd found a cure. Or some way to help. This particular article was about a court case. Some clinic in Switzerland had been taken to court because they'd ended the life of a patient with Alzheimer's. There was some question about informed consent, but the clinic won the case. I couldn't remember the specific circumstances so I had to resort to Google when I reached home after my visit to Oasis.

My search provided more questions than answers. The difference between murder and euthanasia is basically semantic. You still have to kill someone, even if you call it euthanasia. Whether it's a crime or not depends on the country where you happen to be living. It's ethical to kill someone who's terminally ill if you live in Switzerland or Australia, but it's definitely illegal if you happen to be in South Africa. Karl was always moaning that his South African passport complicated his travel schedule, but neither of us anticipated that a local passport would also be an impediment when it came to killing our mother.

You need to have a doctor on your side if you're thinking of euthanasia. It's not easy to kill someone without hurting them. That's why suicide attempts so often fail. You're more likely to end up maimed rather than dead. I couldn't take that risk with my mother. She already walked with a limp. I couldn't consider another disability.

It was inconceivable that I could kill her myself. I couldn't ask Dr. Dave to help me. My mother was more his friend than his patient, after all the years of family consultations. And even if she'd been a total stranger, I couldn't ask him to do it. He'd be struck off the roll. He could even be thrown into prison. And so could I, if I tried to do it on my own.

It's not easy to kill your mother.

It would have been easier if I'd had the foresight to get her written permission. She believed implicitly in mercy killing. She thought everyone should have a living will so the doctor could help a patient avoid meaningless years on life support. But as was inevitable with my mother, she'd never got off her soapbox for long enough to draw one up for herself. She'd told me countless times to push her off a cliff if she got Alzheimer's, but she never wrote it down on a piece of paper.

I did more research on Google. It gave me all the answers, but I couldn't bring myself to make the decision. I tried to deflect the central issue by focusing on the logistics. It was feasible. The right to die is written into the Swiss constitution. You don't need a Swiss passport to get a lethal dose of Nembutal at the Dignitas clinic.

All you need is money.

I looked at my balance sheet. I'd become more adept with figures since I'd started handling the finances at Gabrielle's. I was surprisingly solvent. I paid no rent because I'd lived either with Daniel or my mother. I was well paid at Gabrielle's and M-Net had added to the coffers with my share of *Daniel and Hannah*. But it was my innocuous Lotto win that tipped the balance.

Because I was checking, I opened an account I usually ignored. It triggered a jumble of memories - memory is on my mind The stolen ticket. My mother, perched in expectantly on the couche as we watched the spinning balls. Four not-so lucky numbers. A paltry deposit. Waiting for the future...

I'd never touched the money. It wasn't a large amount, despite the interest it had gained, but prophetically, it was enough to cover the cost of Schengen visas for my mother and me.

I'm not a religious person. I've never had a message from the gods. I knew it was illogical, irrelevant and immaterial, but the fact that I'd stolen enough money to buy a European visa seemed like a seal of approval. I booked two tickets to Zurich. Return tickets. I couldn't come to terms with the possibility that there might only be one of us on the flight back to Cape Town.

➤

TWENTY-SEVEN

I told four people about my decision and only half of them agreed with me. I told Daniel first because he was the only one on the same continent. I knew what he'd say. He's Catholic.

"You can't do that, my darling," he told me as I sobbed onto his shoulder. "I completely understand what you're saying, but it isn't your decision. You can't pass judgment on what her life is worth. You have a whole lifetime of memories of your mother. Her illness is a tragedy, but it's still part of her life. Part of her destiny. You're looking at it more from your own point of view than from hers. You can't bear to watch her suffer, but you have no idea what she can bear. Or even if she's suffering. Maybe it makes more sense to her than it does to you. Perhaps Alzheimer's lets you remember your life as you would like it to have been. Maybe she thinks your father is still with her. Perhaps she doesn't remember that she limps. You can't know what life is like from her perspective. It's not up to you to decide that her life is worthless."

"Don't tell me this is part of some plan," I told him, hunching away from his warmth. "This is illness. Pure and simple. She's not my mother anymore, even if she's wearing my mother's face. I don't know the person she's become. And she's going to get worse. I won't put her in a bed behind bars with a whole lot of strangers. I can't bear to think of what they might say behind her back, when she shouts and swears and says things my mother would never ever say. I can't end it myself because she's my mother. The most I can do for her is to take her to Switzerland."

But Daniel shook his head. Mercy killing is anathema to a Catholic.

"I understand how you feel about putting her in a home, surrounded by strangers. You must both move back here with me," he insisted. "We'll make it work. We'll get a nurse to help us. We can do it."

I shook my head. Daniel and I already had a complicated relationship because we worked together. There were already cracks in the foundation because of my mother's illness. My work suffered because she took up more time than I had to give her. And customers at a restaurant don't care if your mother's sick. They've driven across town to sample Daniel's speciality duck. They don't want to hear that duck is off the menu because his partner didn't place the order with the butcher, that the butcher has become reluctant to deliver any meat at all because she keeps forgetting to pay him. Word of mouth has a ripple effect in the restaurant business. I could damage everything we'd worked for if I didn't do my part.

And work was only one of the ingredients in the recipe. We'd never be alone if my mother moved in. It wouldn't have worked, even before she became ill. A resident mother is a poor addition to any relationship, even if she doesn't have Alzheimer's. I was afraid I would lose both Daniel and Gabrielle's if my mother came to live with us. I couldn't accept Daniel's invitation.

Assisted suicide seemed the most workable solution to an intolerable dilemma. I'm not a Catholic. I can't believe that any god worth praying to would include as cruel a disease as Alzheimer's in his list of human suffering. I can't believe it can be right to sit back and let nature take its course. Not if there's a choice. Engineers are praised when they divert a river from its natural course if it prevents farms from being flooded, if it saves people from drowning every year. My mother was drowning. I didn't have the skills to save her.

But there were doctors in Switzerland who did. And I had access to them. I believed my mother would beg me to find the strength to make the journey.

➤

"I know what Chloe would say," agreed Julia when I made one of my tearful midnight phone calls to London. "I can hear her saying it. She'd say, 'Christ, Hannah! Give me the fucking injection! I even get a jaunt to Switzerland thrown in as part of the deal!'"

We both laughed. Sort of laughed. I could also imagine my mother saying that, almost word for word. But of course, it wasn't funny.

"I think she's right," said Mary when I told her how Julia had reacted to my suggestion. "I'm sure that's what Chloe would have wanted. God, it's what I'd want, if I was her. It broke my heart to see how much she'd deteriorated at Christmas."

I got a lot of support from all my best friends during my mother's illness. Daniel, Julia and Mary. They sound like a pop group. I talked to each of them for hours on numerous occasions, but it didn't really matter what they thought. I didn't need their permission. She wasn't their mother.

But she was Karl's. His opinion carried as much weight as my own.

"You can't do that, Hannah," he said when I phoned to tell him that I'd decided to go to Switzerland. "It's not the same as taking a dog to the vet. I know exactly how you must feel, but this is Mom we're talking about."

I exploded like a bomb flying over Hiroshima.

"You know exactly how I feel?" I asked incredulously. "You have no fucking idea how I feel! You're sitting safely in your fucking commune, milking your fucking Colorado cows!" I felt like adding a few more fuckings, but I needed to get on with the rest of the sentence. "You didn't see those women at the care center. They could be sitting in those chairs for another ten years. Staring blankly. Or screaming. She would hate it. You must know how much she would hate it!"

"Hannah," said Karl. "Calm down. I know it's hard to handle this by yourself, but this is Mom you're talking about. You can't make a decision like this on your own. She's still my mom, even if I'm on a different continent."

"But she isn't!" I said despairingly. "She's not Mom anymore. I know we always complained that she was mad, but that was because we knew she was a million miles from mad. She was razor sharp. She could have made a case for one of her causes in the Constitutional Court. She always knew exactly what she was doing and why she was doing it. And now she doesn't even know who she is. She couldn't bear to be the person she's become. I'm making this choice for her, not for me."

I wondered if this was true.

Karl sounded subdued as the conversation limped along. "I'm not saying you can't do it because I disagree with you," he told me gently. "I know she would hate to be like that. I hate to think of her in that situation. But you won't be able to do it because you're from South Africa. Believe me. I've been traveling for decades. People with a European passport just get on a plane and fly wherever they like. I'm the one who gets stopped at the gates because I need another fucking visa. I'm willing to bet you can't even kill yourself on a South African passport."

I was always in tears while I was trying to kill my mother. Karl and I shouted at each other for another half hour. Then we both went off to check it out on Google. That seemed to be about as far as Karl was prepared to travel in this situation.

>

I became very familiar with the Dignitas website, even though it's a translation from the German. It's a very bad translation. The word order was all wrong. I felt like Alice in Wonderland as I read the broken English. *There are people abroad who read this, the loading judge to be a true view, arriving unannounced and die on the spot want.*

I knew what it meant even though it didn't make much sense. But planning your mother's death doesn't make much sense either. The jumbled words seemed to reflect the way I was feeling.

Karl phoned me back within half an hour.

"I told you, Hannah," he said but he sounded tired rather than triumphant. "They give a whole list of countries linked to Dignitas. I've printed it out. Just shut up and listen. America. Australia. Belgium. Canada, Denmark, Germany. England, France, Israel. Italy. Netherlands, Japan, Scotland and Switzerland. Not a single African country. You'd probably have more chance if you came from Mars."

"But it says there's about fifty-two countries," I protested. "Where's Sweden for example? I can't believe Sweden doesn't support assisted suicide. Dignitas actually markets itself to foreigners. They've even opened a clinic in Germany and they've got the Holocaust to contend with. It says there are no requirements for residency in Switzerland. Or registration or a terminal disease. Patients only have to visit a doctor once to get approved."

"They've tightened that up," protested Karl. "But even if they saw her fourteen times, it wouldn't make any difference. Dementia's not the same as multiple sclerosis. It's not a physical thing like being paralysed. Dignitas can't agree to assisted suicide unless the patient gives consent. There was a huge outcry when they agreed to help that young rugby player who was paralyzed, but it wasn't his parents' decision in the end, although they took him to the clinic. He wanted to do it. He'd tried to do it himself three times before he got there, but the press said that by agreeing to help him the fourth time, Dignitas had suggested that the lives of disabled people are worthless. They can't deal with mental illness once it's taken hold like it has with Mom."

"But I do think her life is worthless with her in this condition," I protested. "And what's more important, I know that she'd think her life was worthless. I've lived with her all my life. I know how she thinks. How she thought. They'll only have to talk to her once, and they'll know she's not thinking coherently anymore."

"That's exactly the point, Hannah. That's why they won't be able to do it. It would open up all sorts of possibilities for exploitation. The patient has to drink the overdose himself. Or pull a lever or whatever way they decide to do it. If the doctors did it themselves, they'd be arrested. And so would you, Hannah. Don't even think of giving her an overdose yourself."

I put down the phone in tears, but I didn't cancel the flights to Zurich. I contacted the clinic and made an ap-

pointment. They didn't want to do it without the paperwork, but I insisted that I had to see them. I was going
to come anyway, even if I had to sit around in the waiting room forever. They couldn't make a judgment on the
strength of a piece of paper. I wouldn't take no for an
answer.

But I had to in the end. I couldn't make even the initial
appointment without the paperwork. "Dignitas is not a
walk-in clinic," they kept saying. They must say it all the
time to desperate people. I was forced to make another
appointment, closer to home. I'd been reluctant to haul
Dr. Dave into a family crisis, but there was no alternative. Dignitas insisted on extensive medical records and a
recommendation from a doctor before their team would
even consider making their own assessment of each individual case.

TWENTY-EIGHT

As usual, I burst into tears as soon as I sat down in Dave's surgery. He'd probably written me off as a chronic depressive. I wept every time I saw him. I sobbed out some garbled saga about my mother. About Mr. Du Plessis and his luckless mother. About my visit to Oasis. The bars on the bed. The patient screaming. About Zurich. He listened with his usual patience, but his body language wasn't promising.

"My dear," he said, taking my hand across the table after I'd stopped waving it in the air. I wondered how many times he'd done that since my mother's illness started. "I understand exactly where you're coming from. I've never been asked to do this before so I'm not familiar with the protocol, but I know about Dignitas and what they aim to do. I would imagine the ethics revolve around the issue of informed consent. And Chloe is no longer in a position to give them that assurance."

More tears. More protests. More waving hands.

"You've known her for so long," I pointed out. "You were the one who gave the original diagnosis. You've watched her deteriorate. Watched her evolve into a different person. One she would most definitely not want to be. You've heard her tell me to push her off a cliff. You're a witness. She's said the same to Karl. That's three witnesses. Surely they'll accept the testimony of three separate adult witnesses? Surely that qualifies as informed consent?"

"*Push me off a cliff* is not the same as informed consent," he told me gently. "It's an emotional response to the diagnosis of a terminal illness. It's also hearsay. It won't stand up in a court of law without a signed affidavit."

"You know it's the truth!" I pleaded. "You know she'd say it if she could!"

"My dear Hannah," he said again, my hand back in the warm comfort of his clasp. "I believe assisted suicide would be Chloe's choice in her circumstances, so I'll write you a letter. I'll collate the records in her file to back up the claim, but I'm not certain that will be enough to get you an appointment at the clinic."

➤

I collected the letter from the surgery the following afternoon. It lurked in my handbag like a ticking bomb all afternoon. I couldn't bring myself to read it until my mother was asleep. I took it to bed with me and lay back on my pillow for a few moments before opening the envelope. I smoothed out the paper and made my eyes read the words he'd chosen to sentence my mother to death.

EMMERSON SURGERY

Practice No 1588777

12 Emmerson Road, GARDENS, Cape Town

Tel 021 671 2792 * Fax 021 671 3540

Dr George Coleridge *Dr Graeme Logie* *Dr David Dunstan*

MB ChB   MB ChB DCH (SA) MB ChB DCH DA MCFP

Consultations by Appointment

Dr P F Hofmeyer

Dignitas

4 August 2011

      I write this letter in response to a request by the adult children of Chloe Cartwright who has been a patient at this practice for twenty-three years. Your official website claims to offer assisted suicide to 'anyone suffering an illness that will lead inevitably to death.' It also states that 'there is no requirement that suffering is confined to the physical.'

      In the light of these statements, I feel that your organization should consider setting up an appointment to see Chloe Cartwright who is in the advanced stage of Alzheimer's disease. In support of this diagnosis, I have attached a copy of the patient's medical history, including the results of the Mini Mental State Examination (MMSE) as well as the relevant blood tests showing elevated homocysteine levels and the existence of two copies of APO-Ee4. I have also included copies of dated CT and PET scans, which have been taken as her illness has progressed. I would like to draw your attention to the following pathological changes which have become more pronounced with each subsequent scan.

Excessive atrophy of the brain.

Loss of cholinergic neurons.

Loss of synapses.

Presence and accumulation of neurofibrillary tangles.

Amyloid accumulation and the formation of senile plaques.

As you will see from the medical records, these physical changes have been accompanied by the other symptoms which characterize severe or late-stage Alzheimer's.

Both short-and long-term memories are severely impacted, with the patient often unable to recognize loved ones or remember large segments of her life.

Her vocabulary is reduced, so she is unable to express her needs.

She is almost constantly in a state of agitation and has become physically aggressive towards her caregivers. She has developed a paranoia about theft and incarceration which makes her a difficult patient for care institutions.

She is incontinent with no control over either bladder or bowel functions.

Her movements are becoming increasingly stiffer and slower. This causes her to become both frustrated and angry.

There is no possibility of Chloe Cartwright regaining either her physical or mental facilities. Her situation is compounded by the fact that, as her records show, the first symptoms of her illness were identified when she was only fifty-nine years old. As is normal with early-onset Alzheimer's, she has deteriorated rapidly. Her mental decline is, however, far more advanced than her physical decline and the illness has been confined to her brain. She is likely to have to continue in this condition for at least another decade which will place her children under great emotional and financial strain as she will require full-time care in an institution.

I have been motivated to write this letter because of my long relationship with Chloe Cartwright, both as a patient and as a friend. From the first consultation when she and her daughter visited me with regard to the symptoms she was displaying, she stated that she would not choose to continue living if her symptoms worsened as they have done. She frequently expressed the same sentiments independently to both her adult children and the three of us would be prepared to testify in a court of law that death would be her choice in the circumstances in which she now finds herself, although she has now progressed beyond the stage when she would be able to convey this wish to a doctor.

I hope the Chloe's irreversible condition and lengthy life expectation as well as her expressed wish to die in these circumstances will persuade you to consider this application in a favorable light.

>

I made copies of Dave's letter for my brother and all my best friends. I locked one copy in my secret drawer so I could take it out and read it whenever I needed to know that there was some substance to what I aimed to do. I fed the original into a large white envelope, along with the bulky medical records of everything the machines had told the doctors as they probed my mother's skull. My hands were shaking as I addressed the envelope.

Dr P F Hofmeyer
Dignitas
Postfach 9
8127 Forch
SWITZERLAND

I paid for a courier service to deliver it to the clinic. I felt as if I'd stabbed my mother in the back as I left the post -office. I couldn't go to work while I was waiting for a reply. I sat around the house and read Dave's letter over and over again.

My heart almost stopped beating when the doorbell rang a few days later, and I saw the courier's van outside the house, a man holding a registered letter addressed to me. I recognized the Dignitas logo on the cover. My hands felt slippery as I signed the delivery note.

My mother was sitting quietly on the sofa in the lounge when I went back inside with the envelope in my hand. I couldn't look at her. I couldn't sit beside her. I couldn't open the letter in the same room. I made my way to the bedroom and closed the door behind me. Opened the envelope with icy fingers.

They had offered me an appointment. The final sentence stressed that an appointment did not guarantee that Dignitas would proceed. The decision would depend on an internal assessment.

I had to try.

➤

TWENTY-NINE

Iris Murdoch's husband advised against travel with an Alzheimer's patient. I could now understand his view, long before our plane took off from Cape Town airport. My mother had always loved airports. She hadn't traveled enough to become jaded and fed up with queues and delayed flights and cramped spaces. She loved the bustle of an airport with its neon lights and signboards, flashing news of flights bound for far-flung places. I realized on the way to Zurich that she didn't love them anymore. She was out of her familiar comfort zone. She looked terrified.

Daniel insisted on driving us to the airport because he felt I couldn't cope with my mother and the luggage and the limp and the Alzheimer's. He shepherded us as far as the check-in, where I requested a wheelchair. He held me tight and wished me luck. I could hardly see him through my tears when he kissed my mother gently. We both knew it might be the last time he'd see her.

"You don't have to do this," he told me softly. "I'll take you both home if you've changed your mind."

My mother looked old and frail and tired. I knew she was frightened by the noise and the lights and all the movement, by everything she used to love about traveling. Alzheimer's was writing an entirely different script for her to follow in the years ahead. I knew she'd struggle to remember the words for this new version of herself. I took a deep breath and told Daniel we were leaving.

The problems started as soon as the hostess arrived with the wheelchair. My mother refused to sit in it.

"Come on, Mom," I said persuasively. "This will be much easier for us." But she pushed me away. The hostess and I both tried again. My mother started shouting.

"Leave me alone!" she cried at the top of her voice. "Stop it! You're hurting me! When are we going?"

Everyone turned round to stare. Whispered comments. She was stronger than she looked as we pushed and shoved. I thought we'd have to call for a straitjacket. I could feel the tears rising in a tide behind my eyes.

"Get in the fucking wheelchair," I muttered. The airhostess looked shocked. Understandably. I shocked myself. The air-hostess would look even more shocked if she knew where I was taking my mother. The tears were pouring down my cheeks by the time we finally got her seated in the chair.

Things looked up a bit after that. There are perks to traveling with someone in a wheelchair. We were promoted to the top of the queue and whisked through customs. We were far too early for our flight. Daniel had warned me that we'd have too much time to kill, but I couldn't bear to hang around at home, waiting until it was time to go. I told the airhostess that I'd take my mother to the Business Class lounge. I'd never travelled Business Class before. The prospect of free sandwiches would have been exciting in other circumstances. A free gin and tonic sounded like a winning proposition after the wheelchair confrontation in the departure lounge.

My spirits felt a great deal better as I helped my mother out of her wheelchair and settled her in comfort in the lounge. She started tucking into the array of snacks and sandwiches I'd brought her. I felt she deserved a scotch and soda.

"I'm just going to wash my face," I told her as I nipped into the toilet. Tears and mascara are never a good combination, I thought ruefully when I caught a glimpse of myself in the mirror, but there was no time for damage control. I willed my bladder to function at the speed of light. I couldn't have been gone more than a few minutes.

Her chair was empty when I came out. I could hardly believe my eyes. It didn't seem physically possible for her to have disappeared in the time I'd been away. She had a limp, for God's sake. How could she have sprinted off the minute my back was turned? I looked feverishly around the lounge, but she was nowhere to be seen. I panicked. I rushed into the gents and accosted some luckless businessman who was in full stream at the urinal.

"Have you seen an old woman?" I blurted. "With a

limp?" I added, as if a whole array of old women might have passed through the men's toilets. He looked at me as if I was mad.

I dashed out again and screeched to a halt in front of the receptionist.

"Did an old woman go out of the lounge?" I yelled.

"She went down in the lift," she nodded. "Is there a problem?"

I felt like ripping open the lift doors like Superman, I pressed the button frantically. "Don't panic," I told myself firmly as the lift descended. She could hardly have made it onto the runway, even if she had been a Springbok athlete. The chances of her being mowed down by a Boeing were minimal, but where the hell was she?

My heart turned over with relief when I spotted her standing at the sweet kiosk. The assistant was remonstrating helplessly with her as she stuffed handfuls of imported chocolates into her pockets. She doesn't have my talent for shoplifting, I thought ruefully as I got involved in a tug of war over the stolen chocolates.

I paid for them in the end. I should have kept one as a memento for my secret drawer, but I'd eaten them all by the time we eventually got onto the plane.

❧

It was a long two hours at Cape Town airport but they were nothing in comparison to what lay ahead on the flight to Zurich. Via Frankfurt. There's no direct flight from Cape Town to Zurich.

I'm surprised our fellow passengers didn't break out

in a spontaneous round of applause by the time we finally landed. The horrors piled up pretty quickly once our charming hostess had settled my mother in her aisle seat. Her name was Suzanne. We would be well acquainted with the unfortunate Suzanne by the time we reached Zurich.

First of all, my mother leaned over and took the leather handbag of the passenger who had drawn the unlucky seat across the aisle from us. I was looking out of the window at the time and was alerted to the crisis by the yelp of protest from the handbag owner. My mother had unzipped the bag with unusual dexterity and was already clutching a large brown wallet. She unleashed a yelp of protest of her own as I grabbed it out of her hand. My mother had never been a quiet type so her version of a yelp of protest was loud enough to make everyone in business class crane their heads to see what was going on. They probably thought it was a hijack. I felt as if we were some sort of in-flight entertainment program that everyone was watching as I wrestled with my mother to try and get the wallet before she started tearing up the money. The charming Suzanne was at our side in seconds.

"Is there a problem?" she inquired helpfully as I tried to resist the urge to knock my mother unconscious with the stolen handbag.

"My mother's not herself," I said helplessly as she yelled with protest when the handbag was returned to its outraged owner. I thought we might both be arrested. It's probably a criminal offense not to declare an Alzheimer's patient at the check-in counter.

I tried to create a diversion with the movie channel. What would she like to watch? I frantically flicked through the channels. I felt as if I'd actually won the Lotto when I came across Shrek in the Golden Oldies section. My mother loves Shrek. I'd bought a copy for my DVD collection after she watched it at home one afternoon. She's watched it at least six times since then.

She seemed calmer once I put the headphones on for her. It must have made the unfamiliar environment seem safer, as the well-loved story played out on the screen in front of her. The rest of the plane is blocked out when you're plugged into a movie.

There's a wonderful book written by an Australian woman with Alzheimer's. Australians seem to be able to handle everything better than the rest of the world. Her name is Christine Boden and I bought the book because of the title. *It's called Who Will I Be When I Die?* which was a question I'd asked on my mother's behalf as I watched her turning into someone I didn't recognize any more. In the book, Boden mentions the wonders of earplugs for anyone with Alzheimer's. Sounds become muted, muffled and distant. No more struggling to keep up with a multitracked world. I could see the tension easing out of my mother's clenched hands as she watched her favorite donkey on the screen.

I thought about how frightened she must have felt at the airport. Being wheeled down the tunnel by a stranger. Hoisted in a lift onto the plane. Surrounded by unfamiliar faces and voices. I felt anguished that I'd sworn at her about the wheelchair, that I'd wanted to hit her over the head with the handbag.

No one asks to have Alzheimer's.

I waved Suzanne away when she loomed up beside us with the drinks trolley. My mother was deep into *Shrek*. I didn't want any diversions. I was quite keen to try the supper, seeing that it was Business Class, but I thought I could live without it, even though the menu mentioned a prawn starter. They were bound to be frozen, I told myself stoically. My culinary standards had risen since I bought a restaurant and moved in with a chef. I thought of Daniel and his darling dogs. I wished he was here to make me see the funny side of the situation. I would have felt better with a dog on my lap.

I'd been nourishing an irrational hope that my mother would watch Shrek over and over for the entire night but it didn't happen. The other passengers settled down in their horizontal beds and my mother started to fidget. Ah ha – she's getting tired. I rang the bell for Suzanne, and we took off her headphones in a gingerly fashion. Suzanne adjusted the seat into sleeping mode and bustled around with a pillow and a blanket. The lights went dim and the conversation died down around the plane. Thank God. I closed my eyes. Prematurely, as it happened, because my mother started to talk.

"When are we getting there?" she boomed into the silence.

"Soon, Mom, "I whispered soothingly. "We'll be there

as soon as you wake up. Go to sleep now."

"When are we getting there?" she insisted. "Late," she added. "We mustn't be late. When are we getting there? Mustn't be late."

I think that's what the white rabbit said in Wonderland. I was starting to feel that I'd moved into Wonderland as a permanent resident. I could hear the other patients turning over as she went on. And on. And on. A jumble of non-stop words, like a breaking dam.

I was desperate.

Suzanne arrived beside us. No doubt passengers were pushing complaining buttons from every corner of the plane. The poor sufferers in Business Class had forked out a fortune for their seats. Now they found themselves subjected to some mad old woman. Suzanne and I were wringing our hands. I'd brought some sleeping pills, but she spat them out. Sleeping pills are so bitter.

"When are we getting there?" she said. "Mustn't be late."

I wanted to die as she continued. I certainly wanted her to die. I wanted to stand up and announce to the other passengers that I was on my way to kill her so they didn't have to worry about the return flight. I suppose she must have stopped talking for a while during the eight hours it took us to reach Frankfurt, but it certainly didn't seem like it. Even Suzanne looked sullen by the time she served breakfast.

I felt like hiding under my seat as the passengers filed past us on landing. Everyone looked hostile as we were whisked past them with the wheelchair and onto our connecting flight. I felt like a zombie by the time we disembarked at the Zurich airport. It was bustling with Swiss efficiency.

Karl was waiting for us at the exit gate. I wept with delighted surprise. And then with despair.

My mother had no idea who he was.

THIRTY

I'll have to go back to Switzerland in different circumstances. I paid scant attention to Zurich and the mountain state I'd wanted to visit ever since my mother read me the abridged version of *Heidi* when I was a little girl. She was usually in a hurry, even when it came to bedtime stories, but I still remember the pictures of snow-capped mountains and cows with bells around their necks.

I couldn't tell you if there are snow-capped mountains with attendant cows in Zurich. I might as well have landed in Timbuktu for all the attention I gave to my surroundings. I was too tired to look out of the window, and I was in tears for most of the journey we made to Dignitas in Forch near the German border.

I was very emotional because Karl had come to join me, in spite of all his reservations. God knows where he got the money to buy the ticket. Perhaps he stole it. Theft seemed to be as much a part of our family ethos as a dash of promiscuity, but we still weren't committed to murder. That's all we talked about as the seventy kilometres flew past on the A1 highway. Karl had hired a car and booked a hotel before he flew out of Denver. He must definitely have robbed a bank, but I didn't bug him for the details.

It was a wonderful relief to have someone else in charge.

"I'm warning you, Hannah," he told me. "They won't let us do this." At least he'd started talking about us. I think he understood how the disease had insinuated its hold on my mother since his visit to Cape Town. The lack of recognition at Zurich airport was as much a blow to him as it was to me.

"They'll understand that we have to do it when they see her," I assured him. That's what I'd said when I contacted the clinic to make the appointment. I was absolutely insistent. "I've brought all her books. I've got photos of her dancing on the table. Giving speeches. They'll have to see that how different her life is now. They'll know it would be cruel to sit by and do nothing to help her."

"They won't want to make any decision that's controversial," said Karl. "Dignitas has had some bad publicity. You must have read it all on the Internet."

I'd printed out a bulky file of articles about assisted suicide from Google. Allegations by an ex-employee that it was more about money than a dignified exit. I'd worked out how many thousands it cost at the current exchange rate – even before factoring in the business-class flights from Cape Town. Someone compared the Dignitas flat to an abortion clinic with graffiti on the walls. Bodies being shunted out in plastic bags. I couldn't believe it was like that, and I didn't care about the money. The situation was so surreal that it seemed like Monopoly money to me.

My hands were shaking when I handed Karl the print-outs which described the actual process.

"I've read these, Hannah," he said as he poured me another glass of Californian wine. He'd had the foresight to pack it in his suitcase when he set off on his last-minute flight to Europe.

We'd settled my mother in bed after we booked into our hotel. She was exhausted after the flight and the sleepless night. I was exhausted too, but I couldn't sleep with all the details that were churning inside my head.

Thank God for my brother. It seemed like a miracle that he was with me. He'd slipped off the pedestal I'd put him on since childhood. I needed more help than an international call when I was trying to cope with my mother. Our mother I used to think bitterly, when I logged out of Skype.

But now he was here. I didn't have to make decisions on my own.

"I could hardly bear to read them," I confessed, piling the well-thumbed articles on the coffee table. This was true, but I'd read them about a hundred times anyway. They described the protocol that Dignitas follows at an assisted suicide. An oral dose of an antiemetic drug, followed thirty minutes later by a lethal dose of Nembuthal. There was another ghastly piece saying that they sometimes used helium gas with a black plastic bag over the patient's head. I hid that article at the bottom of my file. It conjured the obvious link with the Holocaust, especially since the clinic was near the German border.

The most moving article I printed describes the death of Anne Turner who'd elected to die after she was diagnosed with a degenerative disease which would have left her totally dependent on her nurses. Like Alzheimer's in the final stages. Julie Walters made a film about Anne Turner's assisted suicide for the BBC. *A short stay in Switzerland.* Neither of us had seen it. I'm sure I could have found a way to watch it. I was afraid I wouldn't go through with my mothers death if I saw the film. Anne Turner takes the barbiturates and then begins retching and choking. It only lasts for thirty seconds but that sounds an interminable amount of time to watch someone that you love. She then drifts into sleep. Twenty minutes later her body flushes purple and goes pale.

And then she is dead.

"I know you so well, Hannah," said Karl gently. "You'll never be able to forget those thirty seconds. You'll worry forever that she suffered, that you shouldn't have done it."

"I'm sure you're right," I conceded. Those seconds haunted me already, and I'd only read about them applied to a stranger. "But the alternative is worse. I can't watch Mom inching towards death for what could be another five years, given the strength of her heart. I can't bear the thought of her staring at nothing. Incontinent.

She doesn't recognize you, and she loves you more than anyone else on the planet."

"This is a pointless discussion," said Karl "because they'll never agree to do it. It's in that same article about Anne Turner. They took her away from her children and asked her on her own if she was sure she wanted to do it. Then when they brought her back to her family, they told her again. 'If you drink this, you will die.' She has to agree. It's impossible that Mom will understand what they're asking."

But I didn't think it was impossible as I fell into an exhausted sleep in the bed beside my mother's in a small hotel in Forch.

I'd never heard of Forch before. Now I'll never forget it.

>

I didn't notice any graffiti on the walls of the Dignitas clinic when Karl and I helped my mother out of the car for our appointment the next morning. It was a low-profile building. It doesn't look like a tourist attraction, despite the claims on Google. I was too strung up to notice anything, now that we'd come this close. I hadn't confided even to Karl how tenuous the appointment was. I'd lied about virtually every requirement. I had no written proof of informed consent. No psychiatric report. All I was armed with was the conviction that my mother would find her present and future circumstances intolerable. She'd rather be dead than dependent. They'd have to listen to me.

To my amazement, she didn't create a riot when the

receptionist led her off for her scheduled assessment by a doctor. Karl and I were ushered into a room where a man stood up to greet us from behind an orderly desk. I can't remember any details about the room, but I'll never forget his face. It was etched with kindness, in the same way you know that Madiba is a remarkable man whenever you see him on the screen.

"Hannah. Karl," he said in unaccented English as he reached out his hand. "I'm Pieter Hofmeyer."

I felt a sudden surge of hope that he would understand. I'd been bracing myself for rejection, but I knew instinctively that this man would be sympathetic to my cause. And he was. He had what I presumed was my mother's file open on his desk. I took the *Not-So-Famous-Five* out of my tog-bag. I piled up the familiar covers, in the order in which they'd been published. I laid the photographs I'd selected beside them. My bargaining tools. My voice sounded halting as I started the speech I'd been rehearsing every day since I made the appointment, but my voice steadied as I said the familiar words.

He didn't interrupt me. He just listened. Nodded. Smiled sometimes. I knew he understood.

Karl picked up the thread when my speech trailed off into silence at the end. It was almost as if my mother was present in the room as we told Pieter all about her. We told him that it was a different woman that the doctor was examining in the room next door.

He paged through the *Not-So-Famous-Five*. Smiled at the photos. Sighed.

"I'll go through the report when I get it from the doctor examining her physical condition. This will be followed by a panel interview with your mother so that we can assess her from a mental viewpoint as well. This will all take place today. We're well aware of the trauma involved for everyone. The procedure will be set up for tomorrow if we decide that Dignitas would be within its rights to help your mother to die."

Karl and I were filled with hope. And wracked with indecision. Tomorrow was so soon. And then it would all be over. We couldn't change our minds after that. It seemed an endless day as we drank coffee in the clinic café and waited.

Karl held my hand when the summons came and we made our way down the passage to hear what had been decided.

"Your mother's records show irreversible damage to her brain. Our panel's interview supported everything you told us, with regard to the confusion of her mental condition," Dr. Hofmeyer began.

I felt Karl's hand tighten around mine as we faced the doctor across the polished desk. It was going to happen. My mother was going to die. My chest constricted. I couldn't think of anything to say. I forced myself to listen as he continued speaking.

"We are, however, concerned, that your mother's physical condition contradicts the damage to her brain. Alzheimer's is associated with a shutting down of various vital bodily functions. Your doctor pointed out the contrast between her physical and mental condition, but the contrast is more marked than her records reflect."

I found myself forgetting to breathe. What did he mean?

"If we decide to go ahead with the procedure, the Swiss police must be notified as soon as the patient is declared dead by the administrating doctor. The police collect the body and conduct an autopsy themselves. The examining doctor has expressed a concern that your mother's death would not be sanctioned by them. Her physical condition suggests that she is not terminally ill. This is probably related to her age. Our examination suggests that her vital organs are strong enough to keep her alive for as long as a decade."

"But what sort of life would that be?" asked Karl.

I was too frightened to speak.

I'd been terrified that we'd succeeded. Suddenly I was terrified that we might have failed.

"Your mother is a very ill woman," said Dr. Hofmeyer, "but given the current progress with mapping the human genome, a court might argue that there's a reasonable chance that progress could be made in treating Alzheimer's during her lifetime," he continued. "Our panel wasn't unanimous about the issue of legality in her case. Dignitas will be closed down if we break the law. And then we won't be able to help anyone. We have helped Alzheimer's patients in the past. It is a terminal illness so some patients do qualify. If they are physically very frail, or very old, we sometimes go ahead, despite the stumbling block of informed consent. Your mother doesn't qualify on either issue. She's still relatively young. It's the opinion of this panel that vital organs such as her heart or kidneys are not in danger of collapse. Because of this, her life expectancy is better than anticipated. A person in her physical condition would have to give us informed consent for us to end her life."

It was pointless to protest.

You don't need to be a doctor to see that my mother wasn't able to make a decision about whether she wanted tea or coffee, let alone life or death.

THIRTY-ONE

Pieter was kindness itself after he'd refused our request. He arranged for a doctor to meet us at Zurich airport to inject my mother with a sedative before the flight to Frankfurt. Another doctor met us there with a stronger dose for long journey back to Cape Town. She slept the whole way, but I didn't sleep at all.

I was haunted by another report that I'd printed out from Google.

It was about Exit International, a euthanasia group with an Australian base. They don't deal with foreigners, but they were in the news because of comments by the head of the organization, Dr. Phillip Nitschke. He was outraged because the wife of an ex-Quantas pilot had just been sentenced to jail for the murder of her seventy-one-year-old husband. He had Alzheimer's and permission for assisted suicide had been refused by a Swiss clinic. His wife had given him a lethal dose of Nembutal which she'd gotten from South America. Nitschke had given an interview in which he advised patients not to go for a diagnosis if they started to exhibit symptoms of Alzheimer's.

"Don't go to a doctor," he said. "Don't have the tests." He said they should seek assisted suicide as quickly as possible. Once a patient is given an Alzheimer's label, the capacity to make a decision would immediately be called into question.

I knit my fingers pointlessly in my lap. I'd hounded my mother to go to the doctor. Insisted that she try the drugs, even though I knew they couldn't cure her. I told myself I was being irrational and overly emotional, but had I condemned my mother because of my lack of foresight? Condemned her to life instead of death? My thoughts were muddled as I drifted between dozing and consciousness.

I don't really know what I was thinking as I looked down at the sleeping face on the seat beside me.

She looked like herself when she was sleeping. Not a paranoid stranger, shouting and accusing. Suspicious and angry. She was still my mother when she was asleep. Her face was thinner but it was familiar. I still loved her when she was asleep. I thought of the doctor at Dignitas. Kind. Sincere. Shaking his head. Denying me the right to make a choice on her behalf. The choice I believe she would have wanted.

The seats in Business Class are horizontal.

My mother lay flat on her back, her mouth slightly

open. As vulnerable as a baby. My fingers flexed on the edges of the airline pillow on my lap. It's silent in an aeroplane when they put the lights out. Dark and silent. My mother was drugged and worlds away already. Could I lay the pillow gently on her face? Exert a tentative pressure? Could I finish what I'd set in motion when I booked our flights to Zurich?

Could I do what I'd asked Dignitas to do my behalf?

It would have been so easy.

No one would have stopped me.

But I couldn't take matters into my own hands. I put the pillow behind my neck where it wouldn't tempt me. Maybe I was thinking of myself. My own life would change forever if I ended hers. I couldn't slide her body into a rucksack like one of my stolen items. I thought of my mother's strident protests about the death penalty. About the iniquity of a judge who condemned a man to die and then summoned some lowly prison warden to tie the noose around his neck. I'd played the judge, but I shied away from the prison warden role.

There are many cumbersome ways to kill a man.

The Swiss doctors wouldn't carry out the first one I'd tried. I couldn't do the second.

I had no idea what would happen next.

>

THIRTY-TWO

My mother went to bed early the night we got home from Zurich. She looked exhausted as I smoothed the hair back from her face on the pillow and switched off the bedroom light. I looked at my watch. Only half-past eight. I couldn't risk going to bed that early, even though I felt as if I'd been wrung out by a muscular washerwoman with powerful hands. My face was as crumpled as my clothes as I sifted through my DVD collection in search of some distraction.

I was stopped by the cover of *Mar Adentro*. The haunted face of a young man with the Oscar statuette in the left-hand corner. *Best Foreign Film 2004.* Alejandro Amenabar. The brilliant Spanish director was a favorite of movie buffs like my mother. She'd dragged me off to see it when it was on circuit. *The Sea Inside.* I'd forgotten about it. I bought the DVD because I loved the movie. I couldn't remember the details of the story, but I knew it was about euthanasia. I made myself a cup of coffee and pressed play.

It seemed like fate that I had a copy of that DVD on hand so soon after I'd failed to exercise my mother's right to die. It's a stunning movie, even for people who aren't in my situation. It raises all the demons Karl and I had faced during our own short stay in Switzerland. It's a true story set in Spain.

Ramon Sampedro travelled the world as a ship's engineer before he became a quadriplegic after diving into a shallow cove as a young man. He fought a thirty-year campaign in favor of euthanasia. The lawyer who helped him was a young woman who was herself suffering from a terminal degenerative disease, so Ramon was far more than just another case to her. He eventually killed himself by drinking a cyanide solution through a straw, with the help of ten collaborators. Each participant contributed to a step of the ritual, without having enough knowledge of the proceedings to be legally indicted for murder.

He said before he died that if they wished to punish the people who helped him, they would have to cut off their hands because that is all that they contributed to his death. The case became a *cause célèbre* in Spain and his death was shown on Spanish TV. He dismissed his life as time passing against his will.

It's a powerful movie. It made even more of an impact on me when I watched it that night after everything that happened in Switzerland. Ramon's predicament was both identical to my mother's and completely different.

He said a life in his condition had no dignity. Accepting a wheelchair would like be accepting the scraps of everything that had changed about his life when his neck snapped on the sea floor that morning. I thought of Mother's reluctance to get in the wheelchair at Cape Town airport. Ramon complained of being trapped by his total dependency on other people. Dependency that came at the expense of intimacy. There were no private moments for Ramon any more. Not even the toilet.

But their situations were completely different. Ramon was trapped in an immobile body with all his memories of his travels and his passions still intact. He had a close relationship with the people who loved him. Two women came to love him, more than platonically, despite the lack of consummation. The music of the great European composers soared through his bedroom from the radio and the record player. He followed soccer and he wrote poetry. I remember the line he wrote about his lawyer he fell in love with, despite being trapped on his pillow.

I always wish for my death, my lips forever entangled in your hair.

Ramon's life was more meaningful than my mother's when he died, but hers had been more meaningful than his because she'd lived it with such vitality. Until now. Now she was far poorer than him because her mind had gone. She couldn't put together a plan to bypass the restrictions imposed by the law.

I sat staring into space as the movie ended. The final scene was of a friend going to visit the lawyer with whom

Ramon had fallen in love and who had fought so hard to help him exercise his right to die. She'd changed her mind about taking her own life as her degenerative disease progressed. She was sitting in a wheelchair, staring sightlessly at the sea.

When the friend handed her the final poem Ramon had written about their love, she asked "Ramon who?"

I was unbearably reminded of my mother's failure to recognize Karl at Zurich airport.

Ramon's words in the movie confirmed what I thought I believed.

"The person who really loves me will be the one who helps me to die."

Were there any cumbersome ways still on my agenda?

THIRTY-THREE

The Sea Inside has a lot of footage of Ramon's diving accident.

It shows a young man standing on a rock above a sheltered cove. The Mediterranean water is that remarkable azure blue. Crystal clear with gentle European waves lapping on the beach. Ramon tells his lawyer that he was distracted. The camera hones in on a young girl basking on a towel. And then you see him dive. The water is broken on the surface. His head crashes onto the sea floor at an impossible angle. You see him floating upwards. He tells his lawyer that he should have died. He'd heard that you die instantly with drowning. A sweet death he calls it.

That's not how I'd imagined drowning.

There was a poem about drowning in the Matric syllabus. I've never forgotten the title. *Not Waving But Drowning.* Four words to sum up desperation. Drowning didn't sound like a sweet death to me.

Nor did Alzheimer's.

It seemed to me that they might be similar. An Alzheimer's patient might feel as if she's drowning. Everything's distorted. You're not sure if a shape is familiar or hostile. There might be a flicker of something brightly colored. Something beautiful. But you can't grasp it. It shimmers out of reach when you stretch your hand towards it.

Maybe memories are like that when the illness gains control and tangles up the truth in knots. You must feel desperate to break the surface, to take a gulp of air, to make sense of your surroundings. Or give up the struggle and sink to the bottom. Fall asleep at last.

You can't do that if you have Alzheimer's.

Not unless someone helps you.

I couldn't get to sleep after the movie ended, despite the long and draining day. My thoughts became increasingly bizarre. I wondered if my mother might have chosen drowning as her choice of exit. The literary connection would have appealed to her. *The Hours* is another of the DVDs in my collection. Nicole Kidman won an Oscar for her role as Virginia Woolfe, just as Judi Dench was nominated for her portrayal of Iris Murdoch. Serendipity. That's not a word I ever use myself, but my mother often used it in lectures to explain how she chose the plots for her novels.

It seemed like serendipity that I had both those films in my collection. The Alzheimer's link with Iris Murdoch was obvious. I thought of Virginia Woolfe because she drowned. She didn't dive into the sea like Ramon. She walked into a river with stones in her pockets. I wouldn't have thought you could drown yourself like that.

A sweet death?

I had misgivings about drowning as I lay in bed, staring at the ceiling, praying to fall asleep. In desperation, I got of bed and logged on. I keyed in "drowning." I was far madder than a hatter but there was no one to stop me. The person who should have been there was Karl. I never stopped loving my brother while my mother was sick, but I came pretty close to doing that while I sat in front of the computer that night. Why wasn't he there to tell me what to do?

He'd made an ineffectual apology when we went our separate ways at the Zurich airport. He said he felt bad about leaving me to cope on my own. Not bad enough to change his ticket. It really pissed me off. Why couldn't he take her back to Colorado? Why was it always me who had to make a plan? Couldn't he and Pocahontas store my mother in an adjacent wigwam?

My big brother had become unsteady on his pedestal as my mother's illness progressed. I felt very isolated. I had to keep reminding myself that he must have robbed a bank to get to Zurich. How would I have coped with Zurich on my own? He was there when it counted most.

I skimmed through the post that came up on my screen as I sat there in the dark. It's amazing what obscure information you can unearth on a computer when sleep is at its most elusive. I learned that drowning has advantages for anyone looking for the least cumbersome way to kill. Drowning is efficient. That's what I read on Wikipedia. It's almost impossible to prove by autopsy because there's no evidence of a wound or a struggle. The website claimed there wouldn't be a struggle. It's only in movies that drowning people wave their hands and shout for help. A person who's drowning can't shout for help. Breathing is the priority. There's not enough air to breathe so the shouting reflex doesn't kick in. Waving is the same. You can only lift your arms out of the water if you're floating. And if you're floating, you aren't drowning.

Not waving but drowning.

She must have written that before Wikipedia provided all the answers. Perhaps the poem wasn't about drowning after all. I never bothered with more than an opening line because even teachers can't be sure what poems mean. Maybe it was a call for help?

The computer hadn't helped me much. I abandoned the keyboard and went back to bed. I couldn't fall asleep. Had Wikipedia been sending me a message? More serendipity? Maybe drowning would be a sweet death after all? I wondered if I could induce my mother to follow Woolfe's example. What were the chances that she'd walk out to sea if I left her on Fishhoek beach?

No doubt a bloody lifeguard would plunge into the waves.

Perhaps I should run a nice hot bath when she wakes up, I thought. She'd been doing that for Karl and me all our lives in the hope of curing everything from a broken arm to a broken heart. What were the chances that she'd fall asleep and slip quietly below the surface? Maybe a nice hot bath could heal a broken mind as well?

Dreams of my mother's drowning eventually lulled me to sleep.

THIRTY-FOUR

Shoplifting's in a different category from murder, although both of them carry a jail sentence.

Repeat offenders for shoplifting can spend years in jail, even though it seems like petty crime to me. I suppose it doesn't seem like that to the shop owners. Apparently their losses mount up to millions by the time they do a stock-take at the end of a financial year. The courts have to be severe with repeat offenders in a country where crime is as endemic as it is in South Africa. Paradoxically, I think a local court might be more tolerant over a murder motivated by compassion than a first world country like Australia or Canada. We have the most enlightened constitution in the world. The courts might listen more carefully here than in countries where people don't break the rules as much as they do here. Some American states still have the death penalty.

I never found out how much the courts would tolerate

because I was never tried for shoplifting. Or for murder. I didn't have time to drown my mother when I woke up each day. Looking after her was a full-time job. Changing a sodden nappy. Force-feeding chocolate Pro-Nutro. Listening. Not that she said anything coherent. I had to keep my ears on full alert to hear what she was doing. I followed her around. Or she followed me. I don't know which was worse. She wouldn't eat. She kept trying to open doors. I had to lock her in.

This meant everyone else was locked out.

I became a recluse after my return from Zurich. I didn't know what to do about my mother so I turned Pepper Street into a prison for both of us. I ordered my groceries online and had them delivered. Technology makes every-thing possible in the new millennium.

Except for euthanasia, that is. You still need a human to hand over the Nembutal.

Daniel phoned me every day. He came to the house. He had a key so he wasn't deterred by the locked door. He sometimes brought the dogs to tempt me out. He thought I was debilitated by depression because my Dignitas plans had failed. I didn't have an alternative plan. My horizons had shrunk. Even my new sleeping pills weren't strong enough to stop me from tossing and turning and waking early when everything was still dark and uncertain. I had Daniel to thank for my new pills.

"I've made an appointment for you to see Dave," he told me firmly. Daniel knew Dr. Dave, not only because of the integral part he'd played in my recent history. Dave and his wife had been regular customers at Gabrielle's for years. "Julia's mom is coming to look after Chloe so don't even think of saying you can't leave the house," he continued. "You're going to see him, even if I have to call in the police to get you there."

I burst into tears as soon as I sat down in the chair opposite Dave. He'd already phoned me for feedback on the Zurich excursion, but I'd been offhand. Desultory. I'd given him the bare bones of my failure. I'd told him it wasn't convenient when he'd asked if he could visit my mother. He made no reference to my rudeness as he reached out his hand across the table to take both of mine in a reassuring grip.

"You must feel as if you're drowning, Hannah," he said - ironically, in view of my watery dreams about my mother. Dr. Dave had a lot of qualifications after his name. Maybe mindreading was one of them. "It's hard even to imagine what you went through in Switzerland. I think it's harder for a daughter to be in this position than it would be for a spouse. If your father was faced with Chloe's illness, he would have been as old as she is. His life would have slowed down too. He would have had more time to come to terms with it. And when you've got more time, you've got more patience. You're trying to run a business. You've also got a partner to factor into the equation. I can imagine how intolerable this must be for both you and Daniel."

I'm sure he could hardly distinguish my words as I wept the tears I'd bottled. "I dread switching off the light,"

I confessed. "I know I'll never fall asleep. Even when I'm exhausted." I shed a few more gallons of tears as I talked. "I don't know what to do. What must I do?"

I didn't expect an answer. No one had an answer.

"I can't give you a satisfactory answer, my dear," he admitted. "But I do know you can't continue in your present circumstances. I know that Chloe's aggression makes it difficult to accept the idea of a care center, but there is no other viable option. You can't stop living because your mother is sick. You know she's not really angry or sad when she shouts or weeps. Don't mistake this as a cry for help. Her behavior is a symptom of her illness, like the red rash which tells you that you have measles. I'll make some further inquiries. In the meantime, you must get some sleep."

He wrote out a script for some knock-out sleeping tablets. He got up from his desk to put the paper in my hand. "Take care, my dear," he said, putting his arms around me. He felt warm and comforting. Like I imagined a father might feel. I thought about what he said as I drove to the chemist to buy my route to sleep.

I wasn't sure I believed him about my mother's sobs. About her anger. How could he know how she was feeling?

But I stopped wondering when I got home. When you live with someone in the advanced stages of Alzheimer's, you only have time to wonder how you are going to survive another day.

➤

THIRTY-FIVE

Some days had more hours than usual. The one in question dragged on for about a decade. I would have yelled hallelujah when my mother finally went to sleep, but I was afraid I might wake her. I tiptoed barefoot through the house, like a burglar, on my way to the kettle. There were ten minutes of silence.

Sweet silence.

My heart sank when I heard an unmistakeable sound. She was getting out of bed.

"Oh God," I thought despairingly. "I can't bear it."

I heard a shuffle. Shuffle is a sinister sound if your mother has Alzheimer's. Particularly if it's followed by the opening of a cupboard door. That's a recipe for chaos. I plucked up my courage and forced myself to the bedroom door I'd closed so recently. My mother was ruffling through the shelves of the cupboard. Throwing the contents on the floor. Jerseys. T-Shirts. Tracksuit pants.

Everything I'd packed away with grim resignation after the last shuffle episode.

"It's gone," she said blankly. "Must find it. Must find it."

"What's gone, Mom?" I asked her. Again. She'd said the same thing the last time she unpacked the cupboard.

"Must find it! Must find it!" she cried with increasing fervor. At an increasing volume.

The knots tied themselves even tighter in my stomach as I approached her. She smelled as if what she was looking for was a toilet. If I had to rank the trials of living with Alzheimer's, incontinence would be close to the top of my list. I'd learned to bear the smell of urine when I unwrapped her each morning but diarrhea was a bridge too far. I felt myself gag in anticipation. I was rougher than I should have been as I tried to lead her to the bed. She was a big woman so she pushed me aside easily.

"Don't push me! Must find it! It's gone! Must find it!" she repeated, turning back to her task. I flinched as the contents of the cupboard piled up like a jumble sale on the bedroom floor.

"Mom," I said pleadingly, "we'll find it tomorrow. Come to bed."

"Must find it!" she yelled again. She'd run out of options in the cupboard by then. Everything was on the floor. She slotted back into shuffle mode. This time she targeted the wall cabinet in the adjoining bathroom. She opened a bottle of bath salts and emptied it on the bathroom floor. A yellow cascade of Syndol followed. My bottle of tonic. My precious sleeping pills. They didn't scatter because they come in popper packets.

A half-finished popper packet. I'd been wolfing them down like Smarties.

I was tempted. Maybe she'd be less frenetic if I could persuade her to have one? Maybe she'd lie still while I changed her nappy?

"Mom," I said. I took her arm. She let me lead her through the carnage on the floor. It looked as if the room had been ravaged by a gang of hooligans. I steered her back to bed. I popped a pill out of the packet and sat down beside her. "Eat this, Mom," I said. "It will help you sleep." I opened her mouth and put it on her tongue. I held my breath. She spat it out on the pillow. I picked it up and swallowed it myself.

I kept a packet of her favorite sweets on the narrow shelf beside her bed. She liked jelly jubes. I don't know what their official brand name is, but they're soft and sugar-coated. They kept them next to the jelly babies in the garage shop down the road where I bought the newspaper. I always had a packet in reserve in case I needed a bribe.

"Mom," I said alluringly. "Do you want a sweet?" She reached out a hand. "No, Mom," I said firmly. "I'll give it to you when you get into bed." She allowed me to lift her legs and lay her back with her head on the pillow. I handed her a sweet. She popped it in her mouth and swallowed it immediately, as she always does. She loves jelly jubes. I put the packet on her bedside table, beside the popper pack of pills. I popped one out and slid it into a jelly jube.

A green jelly jube. A thin white pill. I felt as if I was loading a gun with bullets.

I paused a moment before handing it to her. She put it in her mouth. I braced myself for her to spit it out. I thought she might bite on the pill, with its bitter taste, its poison. But she was too greedy. She swallowed it without complaint. So I did it again. And again. Almost like an automaton. I don't know how many I gave her. I kept on until the jelly jubes were finished. And then I gave her the empty sweet packet. She was distracted. Like a baby with a new toy. I unsnapped the fastenings on her nappy. I felt like throwing up when I saw the contents. I gritted my teeth as I started the whole ghastly procedure.

"Keep still" I yelled when the nappy twisted over, streaking my hands with effluent. There were yellow stains down her legs and on the sheets. I scrubbed ineffectually with the cloth I'd brought through from the bathroom. I felt the anger rising in my throat. I started to rub harder. As if she deserved to be punished for what she'd done. I must have hurt her because she whimpered like an animal. Like one of the dogs, when you inadvertently stand on a paw.

Like a dog.

The thought made me pause. My heart twisted like the nappy as I registered how thin her legs were, as the rank smell of effluent settled around us like smog. I was swamped by compassion.

None of this was her fault. It was as dreadful for her as it was for me.

"I'm sorry, Mom," I whispered. I rolled up the soiled nappy and threw it away. Wiped the stains from her legs. She didn't resist when I sat her on the chair while I changed the sheet, plumped up her pillow. She lay quietly on the bed as I slid the new nappy under her bottom. Buttoned up her freshly laundered pajamas.

It felt like a miracle. Could the pills be working their magic? Already? Maybe she was merely relieved to be rid of her foul nappy?

I could hardly breathe when she closed her eyes and went to sleep.

It couldn't have been the pills. Not so quickly.

Maybe the day had been as exhausting for her as it had been for me? I was frightened that I might disrupt the miracle by clearing up the squalor on the bedroom and bathroom floors, so I made my eyes stop looking. I shifted my focus to the two pills remaining in the pack. I'd already had the one my mother spat out, but I decided to take the remaining two as well.

I climbed into bed beside her and switched off the light.

I was desperate to go to sleep myself, to forget that tomorrow would be another day.

➤

THIRTY-SIX

She was dead when I woke up beside her the next morning.

I wasn't immediately certain she was dead. I'd never seen a dead person before. She looked just like herself. As if she were sleeping. Her eyes were shut, the white sheet still folded neatly under her chin, exactly as she'd been when I switched off the bedside light the night before, praying I'd somehow fall asleep myself.

"Mom?" I asked tentatively. "Mom, are you awake?"

"Mom?" I asked again, dread snaking through my veins like icy water. My fingers reached out and touched her face, almost of their own volition. They recoiled defensively, like a curling centipede. Was it her coldness? Or the lack of movement?

I panicked. "Mom!" I cried out, a note of hysteria invading my voice, pitching it at a higher tone than usual. "Mom! Are you all right?"

I pulled back the sheet and shook her. Recoiled again, at the stiffness this time? I shook her once again before I knew the truth. My shaking fingers snatched up the cell-phone which I'd left on the bedside table. Just in case. I punched in D. Dial D for Dave. Double D for Dr. Dave.

It seemed a long time before the doorbell rang.

➤

I was too scared to open it. It rang three times before I answered.

"Dave?" I whispered. As if someone were sleeping. As if I was afraid I might wake someone up if I spoke too loudly. As if I might wake my sleeping mother.

I burst into tears as soon as I opened the door.

"I've killed her!" I sobbed. "I've killed her!" I felt an obligation to confess. As if he was a Catholic priest who could offer some form of absolution.

"Hannah," he said gently, patting my back in a fatherly way. Not that I had any idea of a fatherly version of back patting. I've been a bit low on fathers. Maybe I wouldn't have killed my mother if my father had been on hand, if my brother wasn't in a commune on the other side of the world. Family support should be a prerequisite if you have to deal with Alzheimer's.

He led me back into the bedroom. He paused momen-tarily as he registered the chaos prevailing on the bed-room floor. Perhaps he was looking for bloodstains. It looked as if an axe-murderer had passed through. He sat me down in the armchair before he examined my moth-er. Her eyes were already shut, but her mouth was drooping open. I saw him push her chin up with a gentle hand. He propped a pillow on her chest to close her mouth. He didn't pull the duvet over her face which was somehow a relief.

It would have emphasized that she was dead.

"Let's leave her to rest quietly, my dear," he said, turning to me. "Could you perhaps make us a cup of tea?"

I felt like an automaton as he led me to the kitchen, as I switched on the kettle, set out two cups on the familiar kitchen table. Dave let me work in silence until the tea was poured and I sat down beside him.

"Hannah," he started. "I don't know what happened last night, but I can tell you exactly how your mother died. She has been in the advanced stages of Alzheimer's for some time and Alzheimer's is a terminal illness."

I shook my head. I felt compelled to tell him the truth.

"It was me," I insisted. "I did it." I told him how I'd fed her the pills. Hidden poison in her favorite sweets. How I'd betrayed her trust. I hid my face in my hands and sobbed. I was too ashamed to look him in the eye.

He took my hands away from my face. Made me look at him directly. "The pills couldn't have killed her, Hannah. Insomnia is a common symptom in patients suffering from depression. I often prescribe these pills for them. They're vulnerable patients. I wouldn't prescribe pills that could kill them. A normal person like you or me could swallow a whole packet and they wouldn't die. They would certainly fall into an extremely deep sleep, but they wouldn't die."

"But I gave her so many," I sobbed. "I can't remember exactly how many because I wasn't counting, but I'm sure it would have been enough to kill her. I gave her so many. The post-mortem will show how many she swallowed. I know it was enough to kill her."

"There will be no need for a post-mortem, Hannah," he told me in a voice that brooked no argument. "Your mother's system has been in the process of shutting down for as long as she's had Alzheimer's. It would have been highly compromised by now. Anything could have tipped the balance. Strokes are the most common cause of death in patients of her age. In her condition. A cerebral haemorrhage. Arrhythmia. Any subtle dysfunction would cause an irremediable collapse. It's a blessing, my dear. Chloe's earned a blessing and so have you. It's time for all the people who love her to celebrate everything she contributed to our lives."

He took my hand and led me back into the bedroom. He phoned Daniel and whoever else you have to phone when someone dies. He helped me fold the clothes and put them back in the cupboard. He had already cleaned up the mess on the bathroom floor by the time Daniel arrived to put his arms around me. He stayed with us when they came with the stretcher to carry her away.

I put my mother's death certificate in my secret drawer when Daniel collected it for me. It states the cause of death as bronchopneumonia. It's the most common cause of death in patients suffering from Alzheimer's. No one ever queried it.

And maybe it was the right diagnosis. But maybe it was kindness.

I don't think it would be a contravention of the Hippocratic Oath to condone an overdose for a patient who has no quality of life.

THIRTY-SEVEN

Karl flew over for my mother's funeral. So did Julia and Mary. Daniel organized everything. We had a private cremation which was carried out at the same time as the drinks we had at Pepper Street. The house where we'd grown up. We didn't have a service because the only time we ever went to church was for other people's weddings and funerals. We'd been to a couple of christenings when my friends starting having babies, but my mother had been very cynical about people who suddenly turned into Christians a couple of weeks before they needed a church.

It wasn't a gloomy gathering the afternoon my mother was cremated. I almost enjoyed it, in a way. Our house was packed with people, in groups around the lounge and kitchen or clustered in the small garden. It was an affirmation of how many people were connected with my mother. How many people loved her. There was a good turnout of the various professors who'd passed through her bedroom and shared our cornflakes at the breakfast table. We had a lot to drink. There didn't seem to be a need for speeches. We were there because we loved her. We knew we were lucky to have known her, to have had her in our lives. A sense of relief, rather than mourning hung in the air.

My mother had been gone for a long time already.

Karl held me tight when I dropped him at the airport to fly back to Colorado. "You did well, little sister," he told me.

I wondered what he meant as he walked away. Exoneration? I didn't feel exonerated. Maybe her choice would have been entirely different. Maybe I was wrong. Maybe Daniel was right. And I can't evade the other question.

Did I want her death for her or for me?

I still struggle to fall asleep. Perhaps I'm afraid of the answer.

✄

I proposed to Daniel the night after my mother's funeral, but he said no.

"No?" I said incredulously. "You're saying no? I thought you wanted to marry me? You've always said you wanted to marry me. How can you say no?"

"My darling Hannah," he said calmly. "Today was your mother's funeral. You're emotional. It's not the right day to be thinking about marriage."

"It is the right day!" I insisted. "It's exactly the right day. I was muddled before today. I haven't thought clearly for years. I don't think I've ever seen everything as clearly as I do today. I know exactly who has got me through the last few years. I know exactly who I want to marry."

"Hannah," he said gently." I don't want you to marry me because you're grateful. I don't want you to marry me because I loved your mother.

"But I don't," I said. "I want to marry you because that's what I want. Because I love you. Because I want to get back into your bed. I'm sick of sharing a bed with my mother. I want to have sex. I can hardly remember what sex is like. I need you to remind me."

But he shook his head.

"All right." I said. "I'll admit it. It's not really you I want. It's the dogs. I want unlimited access to the dogs..."

He laughed but he didn't waver. "I'm not saying no," he said. "I'm saying slow. Take it slowly, Hannah. There's no hurry."

I might as well have been pleading with the Rock of Gibraltar. I had to accept it.

➤

We're still not married.

Daniel was talking about a marriage certificate when he told me to take it slowly, but he could have been talking about a death certificate. Winding up a deceased estate takes forever in South Africa. Especially if the deceased is someone like my mother.

The lawyer handed me a list of the documents he'd need to finalize the process. Locating them proved almost impossible. I'm sure the British would have found the Enigma Code easier to decipher than my mother's filing system. I was amazed to come across a valid will. It's ironic that someone with a financial history as precarious as my mother's could turn both her children into millionaires. Our house on Pepper Street was a major piece in the jigsaw of our past. We didn't anticipate how it would impact the future.

"You might as well sell it," Karl had said. "You're living with Daniel and I'm on a separate continent. Neither of us is ever going to live there again."

The estate agent's eyes lit up like a torch when she saw the address. "I know this house! It's the ramshackle one on the corner!"

"Ramshackle?" I said in icy tones. I felt offended on the house's behalf. On my mother's behalf.

The agent backtracked immediately. "I meant quaint," she said. Estate agents are a mendacious bunch. Everyone knows they mean *ramshackle* when they describe a house as quaint. She hurried on to describe its other virtues. It only had one virtue, but it was the one that mattered most.

"Position! Position! Position!" she chanted like a mantra. Cape Town's CBD was expanding in the way that cities always do. There was no more space in the center so the fringe became upgraded territory. Our house was surrounded by newer buildings. Apartment blocks. Restaurants. Offices. I would never feel jealous that another family had moved into our house because it would be demolished before the ink had time to dry on the deed of sale.

I didn't know what to do with the furniture.

"Sell it," said Karl. His new-found wealth had obviously gone to his head. Perhaps he wanted to buy a meadow for the commune. Or a herd of pedigree goats.

But I couldn't walk around our house and stick price tags onto our furniture. No one would want it anyway. Our house always looked like a second-hand junk shop. I phoned the Salvation Army. They said they would come and collect it in a truck. They said the poor would be delighted.

Daniel dropped me off at the house on the day they were scheduled to collect it. I wanted to be there when they loaded up the truck. I must have driven the Salvation Army to distraction because I kept changing my mind about what I wanted to keep.

"You can't take that," I said as they lugged my mother's couch onto the verandah where I was sitting like a harpy, keeping an eye on the proceedings.

"Actually, you might as well take it," I said after they'd maneuvered it back into the lounge through the narrow door. I knew the couch would clash with Daniel's elegant, minimalist furniture. I burst into tears when I saw the look on the collective face of the Salvation Army.

They were lovely men. The driver poured me some tea from his flask. Another one gave me a biscuit. They patted my back and told me they understood as they loaded my past into their truck and drove away.

I phoned Daniel to come and fetch me. The only piece of furniture I'd kept was the little bedroom dresser which held my secret drawer. I opened it and sifted through the contents while I waited for him to arrive. Everything was there. The music box. Julia's tiny ballet shoes. A miscellany of sexy underwear. The red silk dress. And the most recent addition: my mother's death certificate. I have no idea why I put it there. It should have been safely in a file. I smoothed the paper and slid the door closed when I heard Daniel's car in the drive.

He helped me carry the dresser to the car. We both went back inside to check that nothing had been overlooked.

"It's so empty," I said. "I can't decide if it looks bigger or smaller. It certainly doesn't look like home." I can imagine how plaintive I sounded. Daniel came over and held me tight against his warm chest as I wept into his shirt.

"Darling, Hannah," he said into my hair. "It's the end of an era. As if we're starting a brand-new chapter." He loosened his grip. Pushed me an arm's length away, his hands firm on my shoulders. Eyes in sync.

"To have and to hold?" he questioned.

"Till death us do part," I said without a moment's hesitation, my arms in place around his neck.

Maybe that's as married as we'll ever be. It's enough to secure our future.

➤